CONOR'S CAVEMAN

CONOR'S CAVEMAN

THE AMAZING ADVENTURES OF OGG

WRITTEN AND ILLUSTRATED BY
ALAN NOLAN

THE O'BRIEN PRESS
DUBLIN

FOR THEO,
AND FOR SAM, THE EXPERT LISTENER

First published 2015 by
The O'Brien Press Limited
12 Terenure Road East,
Rathgar, Dublin 6, Ireland

Tel: +353 1 492 3333;
Fax: +353 1 429 2777

Email: books@obrien.ie
Website: www.obrien.ie

ISBN: 978-1-84717-732-2

1 2 3 4 5
15 16 17 18 19

Editing: The O'Brien Press Limited

Printed and bound by Norhaven Paperback A/S, Denmark.

The paper used in this book is produced
using pulp from managed forests.

CHAPTER ONE
ICE COLD NEAR ANNAMOE

Conor Claypole Corcoran was a quiet sort of boy. He was the sort of boy who wouldn't say 'boo' to a goose. Let me explain: even if it was Hallowe'en and he was all dressed up with a sheet over his head pretending to be a ghost, and the door he bing-bonged on the doorbell of was opened by an actual goose wearing a cardigan, smoking a pipe and holding a large, tempting wooden bowl of fizzy jellies and fruity chews, he still couldn't bring himself to say 'boo'.

Mind you, that's a pretty unlikely scenario. It has probably only happened in real life one or two times. Three at most. Whoever heard of a goose smoking a pipe? A cardigan I can understand – especially for Canadian geese. Canada can be chilly – but a PIPE??

I think gooses (or 'geese', if you must) on the whole prefer chewing bubblegum to smoking pipes. It explains the large amount of dried-out bubblegum found on the roofs of bus shelters.

And those pink, round things you see floating up high in the sky from time to time – escaped weather balloons? Nope. Gooses (or 'geese'. Sheeze! Have it YOUR way!), GEESE, blowing bubblegum bubbles as they fly north for winter. Or south, if they fancy a sun holiday instead.

But where was I? Oh, yes. Conor.

SSSSSHHHHHHH!!! Did you hear that?

Neither did I: it was the sound of Conor not saying very much.

He really was a quiet chap.

And, unfortunately for Conor, being quiet was a personality trait that didn't help much in scouts, especially at meal times. 'Who wants a sausage?' the shout would go up. 'Me!' 'Me!' 'Me!' the scouts would cry, each one competing to be the loudest, to get the juiciest, most succulent sausage they could. But from Conor? No sound at all. Not a sausage. Which, incidentally, is what he usually got for his dinner on scout trips: zero sausages. He was too quiet and shy to speak up, so he went hungry instead.

Or at least, he would have gone hungry if he hadn't learned the first rule of scouts: to **be prepared**. Before every weekender he packed into his capacious rucksack his toothbrush, his pyjamas, his slippers, his knife and fork and spoon and plastic dish, his compass, his pillow, his yoga mat, his sleeping bag, his flashlight, his shovel and his map. And because he was a conscientious scout who remembered the scout motto (and because he didn't want to starve), every week he also packed sandwiches, bars of chocolate and cartons of juice that he ate and drank by himself. Quietly, alone, and in a corner, like a little mouse. A little mouse with a very quiet squeak.

It was on one of these fairly food-free scout weekenders that our story began.

A trip to Lough Dan! Up in the lovely Wicklow Mountains! Two days away from home and, more importantly, homework! Two days of outdoor fun filled with games, sing-songs and sunshine!

At least, that was what it would have said in the travel brochure, if the scouts had one. (Spoiler alert: they don't.)

The reality was a bit different. Lough Dan was there alright, and it looked lovely. Or at least it would have looked lovely if you could have actually seen it through all the rain.

It was PELTING down; had been since they got there. The moment the last of the convoy of mums and dads performed a seventeen-point turn, beeped the horn and waved goodbye to the precious cargo they had safely delivered (i.e. their kid), the heavens opened and the scouts all ran for cover. And it wasn't just normal rain. It was the kind of rain that made you suspect that evil, child-detesting hobgoblins were hiding in the trees, pouring down buckets of icy water on unsuspecting, innocent juveniles.

The familiar shout of 'ALL HANDS ON DECK!' went up, and the scouts very reluctantly left the imperfect sanctuary of the trees and started to hammer in pegs and erect their tents.

Conor kept his eyes on the tree branches for hobgoblins as he (quietly) hammered in the tent pegs, freezing-cold water dripping down his neck and soaking his scout shirt. Ah, the outdoor life!

Once the three tents were up, all of the scouts took shelter in the girls' one, shivering and shuddering with the cold.

Their scout leader, Dennis Deegan – a tall, skinny Corkman with a big head of unnatural-looking orange hair that Conor suspected he ordered from a catalogue – looked at them with squinty eyes. 'Ye bitter get used to bean in here, gurls and byes,' he said, smirking as he did so. 'Shur, I wouldn't send a dog out on a day like dis …' His eyes glinted. 'Conor! Run out to the car there and get my tea flask!' He flung his keys at Conor, who yelped (quietly) as they narrowly missed his head.

'Mr. Deegan!' cried Charlie Finch, a smallish girl with freckles, a furrowed brow and a missing tooth, as she stuck her chin out like a weapon. 'You can't send Conor out in that rain!'

'Ah, sure, Conor doesn't mind it. Do yeh, Conor?'

Conor, being Conor, said nothing.

'You see? Out ye go, Conor, and don't be there til you're back.'

Conor did as he was told.

Charlie seethed, embarrassed for Conor. She fancied the strong, silent type, and as Conor was one of those things, she supposed she half-fancied him.

'Look at it this way, cupcake,' said Damian Deegan, a lanky boy of twelve with a weasel face. 'Some people are born to be a general, giving orders, and some are born to be the privates who follow them. Conor is just one of those privates.'

'If you weren't the scout leader's son, I'd bash YOU in the privates,' snarled Charlie. 'Lay off Conor!'

Damian's sidekick, Gulliver Quinn, a huge lad for twelve, with broad shoulders and a scout shirt that looked like it was two sizes too small for him, grunted and giggled at the same time – I suppose it would be called a 'griggle'. Damian looked around at him sharply, and Gulliver stopped griggling immediately; he put a finger to his slightly blue-tinged lips to silence himself. 'Sorry, Damian,' he said. 'Won't happen again, Damian.'

'Come on,' said Damian, 'we're going. Dad's gone to the boys' tent already and the smell of perfume and scented candles in here is horrible.'

A few minutes later the tent flap opened, and Conor came in holding a red tea flask and looking like he had been swimming in the lake. He wiped the rain from his eyes.

'GET OUT!' shouted the girl scouts in unison – all except Charlie, who looked apologetically at the half-drowned boy and silently mouthed, 'Sorry.'

Conor, again, did as he was told.

CHAPTER TWO
A BEAUTIFUL NOISE

The next morning, the scouts woke to the thunderous sound of heavy rain on the canvas roofs of their tents. Conor opened one eye sleepily, only to be greeted by the round mound of Gulliver Quinn's pyjama-clad bottom. Despite his large size, Gulliver had wriggled around in his sleep until he was head first in his sleeping bag, with his sizeable backside sticking out the top. Sticking out the top and sharing pillow space with Conor's face.

'Yeeee-uck,' whispered Conor quietly. But not quietly enough. **PAAAARRRRRRRPPPPPPP!** went Gulliver's bum. The beast had awoken! The other scouts, roused by the horrendous noise of flabby bum cheeks flapping together, scrambled out of their sleeping bags and ran from the tent. They would prefer to be on the side of a mountain in a downpour than in an airless tent surrounded by pongy, greeny, eggy gas. And I, for one, can't blame them. A rude awakening indeed.

After breakfast (Conor had a bowl of dry cornflakes and half a sausage that someone had left behind them on their plate), scout leader Dennis ran his hands through his big orange hairdo and daintily picked his nose with the tip of his little finger. He reached over and pulled the tent flap aside. It was still scuttling down with rain.

'Right, so,' he said, standing up and looking at his clipboard. 'Sittle down, lads and lassies, and lissen up. We're only here for the one day, so we're goin' to make the most of it. We're doing orienteering, and I'm going to be splittin' ye up into teams of four, two gurls and two byes on each.' He went down the list of names on the clipboard and named the teams. 'And last but not least, Damian (grand lad, stand up straight now), Gulliver Quinn, Charlotte Finch and Conor Corcoran.'

'That's the way, Dad,' said Damian. 'Two boys on each team, and two girls. Isn't that right, Conor?'

Charlie – who, by the way, hated being called Charlotte – squinted at Damian and growled, but she did it quietly so Dennis wouldn't hear. Damian heard it though, and took a half step behind Gulliver. She may have been a girl, but everyone knew Charlie was one tough cookie.

'This is what I want ye to do,' continued the ginger scout leader. 'I want yis to take one of these' – he held out four different-coloured flags – 'and do ye see that peak up there?' He opened the tent flap again, and they all peered out. Dennis stuck his hand out the tent opening and pointed almost directly upwards. 'Do ye see it?'

The scouts all looked up. Through the heavy multitudes of falling raindrops, they could just about make out the outline of the hill rising up from Lough Dan. The bit that wasn't covered in thick cloud, that is.

'That's where I want yis to go,' said Dennis. He took his arm back in; it was dripping wet.

'Team A, you take the northern route up, Team B the western, Team C the eastern path, and Team D …' He winked at his son, Damian. 'D for Deegan, what? Good man, shoulders back. Team D will take the southern route.'

Dennis threw some maps at the four teams. 'The routes are marked on the maps. Have ye all yer compasses?'

The teams nodded.

'Grand, so. And remember to be back by three o'clock – yer mammies and daddies are picking ye all up then. I'm going back to me sleeping bag.'

The teams pulled on their windcheater jackets, put up their hoods, tightened the strings under their chins, and very … slowly … and … very … reluctantly … they set off on their task. Damian's team (Team D for Deegan!) were the last to leave.

Conor and Charlie's jackets were both a bit threadbare and covered in patches – only a few of which were scout-achievement ones. They weren't great for keeping out the rain, but they pulled them on anyway. Damian's jacket was much fancier. His dad, as well as being scout leader, was a stockbroker, dealing in stocks, shares and big-money deals. He used to be one of those guys in the stock exchange shouting, 'Buy! Buy! Buy!' and 'Sell! Sell! Sell!', but nowadays he worked from home on his laptop. And you couldn't blame him. If you had a house as big and fancy as Dennis Deegan's, you would never want to leave. In fact, the house was so gi-normous, it would be hard to find the way out without a map. Which is maybe what drew him and his son to join the scouts – they needed to learn orienteering and compass skills to find the kitchen.

Damian pulled up his hood and lowered its infra-red visor over his eyes. He clicked the button on his sleeve to activate his jacket's battery-powered central heating function, then sighed in satisfaction, happy in the knowledge that not one drop of rain, icy cold or otherwise, would get through the Teflon microfibre of his coat's lining. No matter how wet it got outside, inside his jacket he would be as dry as the desert and as warm as toast.

Gulliver Quinn didn't put on a coat at all. Conor and Charlie had actually never seen him wear one, and both doubted that he actually owned a coat of any kind. He was just too tough to wear one. Or maybe too thick. Either way, he marched off up the hill without even looking at the map.

'The other way, Gulliver!' shouted Damian sharply. He looked at his compass and gestured for Conor and Charlie to follow him. 'Come on, come on. I have the flag, I'm the leader. The southern route is this way. Let's get this over with.' He turned to look at them. 'And keep behind me, Conor, won't you? I don't like being downwind of poor people.'

Wearing their rucksacks, they all trudged along the steep, muddy path that marked the southern route up the hill. The rain had eased off a little, but the path was still very slippery. Charlie fell a couple of times, prompting Damian to snicker quietly. (He may have been an arrogant twerp, but he knew better than to laugh out loud at Charlie's misfortunes.) Conor was more sure-footed, hopping from rock to rock to tuft of grass like a mountain goat and helping Charlie to her feet when she slipped. Gulliver simply marched upwards in a straight line, walking right through heather and gorse bushes with his eyes on his compass. Every so often he took a bottle of ink from his scout trousers and took a quick swig. Weird thing: Gulliver had gotten a taste for ink after drinking a bottle by mistake back when he was a greedy five-year-old; now he spent almost all his pocket money each week on ink. His favourite flavour, sorry, colour, was called Japanese Blueberry. He wiped his mouth with his hand after each gulp, leaving long, blue (berry) streaks across his fingers and up to the sleeve of his navy scout shirt.

Mercifully, the rain stopped completely as Team D reached the halfway point, and they paused to take a breather and look down at the lough. They were pretty high up on the side of the hill, and the view was spectacular. The sun, much to their surprise, came out from behind a dark cloud, and its faint rays played across the ripples in the water far below.

'You know what?' said Damian. 'I believe Gulliver and I may stop for a spot of lunch.' He handed Conor the red-and-white flag from his rucksack. 'You two keep on going – we'll wait for you here. Gulliver, the picnic blanket!'

As if from nowhere, Gulliver produced a tartan picnic blanket, waved it around his square-shaped head with a theatrical flourish, and spread it out on the ground. Damian sat down on it with a sigh and started laying out the contents of his rucksack: a flask of tea, some hard-boiled eggs and half a roast chicken. Conor's stomach started to rumble.

'Keep that noise down, can't you, Corcoran? We don't want you to cause a landslide, now do we?' He waved his fingers to dismiss them. 'Now then, tiddle-ee tiddle-oo with you.'

Damian nibbled daintily on a chicken leg with his little finger sticking out and threw a boiled egg towards Gulliver, who caught it in his mouth like a large, hungry Labrador. 'And don't forget to stick that flag in the top of the hill when you get there. My dad will be checking from base camp with his binoculars.'

Conor and Charlie kept on going, figuring that they didn't have any choice – after all, Damian WAS the group leader, as well as being the scout leader's son. But that didn't stop Charlie from calling him every bad name she could think of (and inventing new ones) with every step she took up the steep slope. 'Stinky doo-doo snots' was the most imaginative.

Conor thought he could actually see steam coming out of her ears, but it may have been the mist that seemed to be coming down on them as they climbed. Another fifty metres up and the mist had become a thick fog.

Charlie stopped giving out as she noticed that she could only just about see Conor, who was no more than a couple of steps ahead of her. 'Hold on, Conor,' she said. 'This fog is too thick. I think we're going to get lost.'

'Well,' said Conor, 'the summit of the hill has got to be upwards, so if we keep going up we'll get there eventually.'

As much as she loved arguing, Charlie couldn't argue with that logic. And besides, she was much too surprised to argue – other than the rumbling stomach, that short sentence was the first sound she had heard Conor make all weekend.

'Shut up. You talk too much,' she said, and they started up the slope again, moving carefully through the dense fog.

Just as Conor had predicted (there were no flies on this boy), they eventually reached the top of the hill, emerging from the mist into beautiful, warming sunshine.

'That fog was as thick as Gulliver,' laughed Charlie, relieved to have reached the summit in one piece. 'I think we're the first to get here! Yay, us! Let's plant this dumb flag and get back down.'

They propped up the red-and-white flag with stones. 'Dennis will never see it from down there at base camp,' said Conor. 'That fog is too thick.'

'I thought I told you to be quiet,' said Charlie with a smile. Conor smiled back. 'But you're right, Deegan will never see it. It looks like only the very top of the hill is poking through the fog.' She took out the map. 'Now, which way do we go for the southern route?'

They looked around the top of the hill, rubbed their chins and pointed in opposite directions. Charlie took out her compass. The needle was spinning wildly. 'Hmm. I think the battery in my compass is flat. This way!'

Before Conor could explain to her that compasses don't take batteries, Charlie had marched down into the fog. Conor gulped and followed her.

If going up a mountain in fog seemed foolhardy, going down a mountain in fog was downright dangerous, especially as the fog seemed even thicker as they descended. 'Conor! Give me your hand,' barked Charlie. 'I don't want to lose you!'

Conor did as he was told, yet again – and willingly this time. It was very nice to hold hands with Charlie. She was the first girl (apart from his mum) that he had ever held hands with.

They kept their eyes on the ground in front of them as they came down, but even so they stumbled a few times and slipped on loose shale. Charlie looked again at her compass as they walked. The needle was still spinning around like a demented breakdancer. Conor peered at the compass. 'Wow,' he said. 'We're really los–'

But that was as far as he got into that particular sentence – only his third of the whole weekend – because at that moment Charlie's foot caught on a rock and she fell head first into a gorse bush. Since Conor was holding her hand, he was pulled along behind her, and they both ended up in the bush's scratchy, thorny branches.

'Oh, brillia–' began Charlie, but it must have been a day for starting sentences that were never going to be finished. Her words were drowned out by a loud rumble and then a loud **crrrackkkkinngg** noise, as the ground suddenly gave way beneath their feet, and Conor and Charlie found themselves falling through the air into darkness.

It wasn't a long fall, you'll be glad to hear – after two metres or so, they landed on a reasonably soft, soil-covered floor. Half a gorse bush fell with them. 'Ouch,' said Conor. 'Are you okay?'

'I think so,' said Charlie.

They both looked up at the light source above, the foggy hole they fell through. They could see the other half of the gorse bush silhouetted in the jagged circle of light. They looked back at each other and could see their breath in front of them.

'We're in a cave,' said Conor.

'So … cold …' shivered Charlie, her teeth chattering.

'So dark, too,' said Conor. 'Oh! But I have a flashlight!'

He fished through the pockets of his scout shorts for a torch. Aha! He switched it on, and the cave lit up with its bright beam of light. The underground chamber they had fallen into was narrow and tunnel-like, with a sharply sloping floor, and when the two friends tried to get up they found that they were standing at an angle. A few stalagmites hung down from the cave's roof. Or where they stalactites? Conor could never remember. Actually, he was pretty sure that stalactites hung down. Either way, they were creepy looking, like monsters' teeth.

Conor shuddered and swung his flashlight's beam around the stony sides of the cave. Sheer rock wall, sheer rock wall, sheer rock wall (you know, it's going to be really hard to get of here), sheer rock wall, huge hunk of ice, sheer rock wa– Hold on. Huge hunk of ice?

Conor and Charlie looked at each other and patted the dust off their scout uniforms. They walked in torchlight over to the hunk of ice.

'Ice?' said Conor.

'Oh! We did this in geography! This is a whatyoumaycallit! A glacier!' shouted Charlie excitedly, her voice echoing around the cave.

'But glaciers melted thousands of years ago,' said Conor.

'I suppose it's probably cold enough in here to keep this bit frozen,' said Charlie. 'It's only a small glacier.'

'It's not THAT small,' said Conor, running the light of his torch over the ice. 'It's at least a couple of metres tall! It looks like it's attached to the rock wall on this side.' He peered closer. 'There's something frozen inside!' He shone his flashlight at a long, dark-brown shape inside the ice. 'It's a stick. No, it's more like a pole …' He followed the pole shape upwards with his flashlight. 'And it's got a piece of stone attached to the top. It's a … **HOLY MOLEY!!'** Conor jumped back from the glacier as if he had been electrocuted.

'What did you see??' asked Charlie, alarmed.

'Eyes,' said Conor.
'I saw **EYES** …!'

CHAPTER THREE
SLIP SLIDING AWAY

Conor and Charlie crept slowly back towards the huge hunk of ice. They could feel the cold coming off the surface – the closer they got, the colder they became, and their breath hung before them in clouds of mist. Conor wiped at the ice with the sleeve of his weather-beaten jacket. There was the wooden pole alright, looking for all the world like the shaft of a spear, and beyond that, further back in the ice … a pair of blue eyes!

The eyes were attached to a large face, a face with a big, wide nose and a massive, stubble-covered chin. Above the eyes was a big, bushy unibrow that looked like a frozen black furry prehistoric caterpillar.

'Is that ... a MAN's face?' asked Charlie.

'I *think* it's a man,' said Conor. He had his own face pressed up against the icy surface, training his flashlight on the figure inside.

'Is it ... alive?'

Conor looked at Charlie and frowned. 'Hard to tell, but either way – he must be chilly in there.'

The figure in the ice had long, matted hair and seemed to be wearing rough, shaggy animal furs. His hairy, bare arms stuck out of the furs, and he held the shaft of the stone-headed spear in one of his meaty hands. Conor thought he looked just like the drawings of cavemen that they had in their school history books.

'Charlie, this must be a caveman!' Conor searched frantically in his rucksack. 'Maybe he was flash-frozen in a storm during the stone age – you know, like factories do with frozen peas. Maybe he was caught unawares?'

He found what he was looking for – his history book! He had an exam coming up, so he had brought it along to cram during quiet moments over the weekend. He pulled the book from his rucksack and flicked quickly through its pages until he found the section on the stone age. 'Look, Charlie! Stone Age Man – it's this guy! It's got to be!'

Charlie stared at Conor, goggle-eyed. 'Conor Corcoran, this is the most I've ever heard you speak in one go!'

'But Charlie, this is HUGE! A real caveman, frozen in ice, and WE found it!' Conor was back in his rucksack again, searching for something else. When he emerged, he was holding a small metal pickaxe with a wooden handle. Charlie's eyes narrowed. 'A good scout has to be prepared for every eventuality,' said Conor. 'We have to get this guy out of here!'

The problem was, Conor had no idea how to get the huge block of ice out of the cave. It must have weighed a couple of tonnes, and they would need to winch it up through the hole they had fallen through. Not that the hunk of ice had any chance of fitting through! It was, as I have pointed out (for those of you paying attention), pretty huge.

Undaunted, Conor clambered onto the block of ice. Or at least he tried his best to clamber – ice, being ice, tends to be fairly slippy. After three or four attempts, he turned to Charlie. 'A little help here?'

She sighed and laced her fingers together, giving him a bunt up onto the huge hunk of frozen water. He whacked his pickaxe deep into the surface of the ice and hauled himself up to the top.

'The ice is attached to the cave wall, so if I can just chip away with my axe right here …'

Conor lifted the tiny axe and gave a gentle tap at the point where the ice met the stony cave wall. There was a gigantic tearing noise, and suddenly the whole cave started to shake. Dust and small stones started to fall from the ceiling of the stone chamber. The huge hunk of ice lurched suddenly, and Conor dug his pickaxe into the side, holding on tight. Charlie squealed as the ice started to move, slowly at first, wrenching itself away from the stone cave wall it had clung to for thousands of years.

'Conor! **WHAT HAVE YOU DONE?!**' shouted Charlie, flattening herself against the opposite wall of the cave. The enormous slab of ice was sliding down the wall now, picking up speed, with Conor still hanging onto his axe on top.

'I only gave it a tap,' whimpered Conor.

His quiet voice could barely be heard over the roar of ice on stone.

There was a massive **WWHHACCKKK!** as the ice slid completely off the wall and hit the floor. Conor, still holding tight despite the impact, bucked up like a rodeo rider on a bull and found himself in a sitting position, his bottom numb with the cold.

The ice started to slip on the sloped floor. 'Uh oh! We're moving again!' shouted Conor.

Charlie backed away from the huge slab of ice, which was coming straight towards her, sliding easily on the angled floor. But there was nowhere to move out of its way – the tunnel-like cavern was too narrow. She broke into a blind, panicky run.

'I can't stop it!' wailed Conor. 'There are no brakes!'

The ice slid faster as it gained momentum, and Conor could see Charlie running wildly in the darkness in front of it. He knew that if the block caught up with her, she was going to be squished. Without thinking about it too much – which, given the circumstances, was probably quite a good thing – Conor stuck his flashlight between his teeth, and, hanging on to his pickaxe, which was still jammed into the ice, he inched forward on the block, his remaining hand reaching out for his friend.

The huge block of ice was easily outpacing Charlie, who was running in the dark, not knowing if she was going to trip on a stalagmite (or were they stalactites that grow up from the floor? Like Conor, Charlie wasn't 100% sure about that either) or hit a rock wall at any moment.

Then three things seemed to happen at once. Let's see if I can describe them. The first thing that happened was that Charlie DID trip, but not on a stalagmite or even a stalactite – she tripped on a plain old rock, and she started to sprawl forward into the darkness with her arms flailing. The second thing that happened was that Conor got himself far enough forward on the rapidly moving block of ice that he was able to reach for the back of Charlie's coat tail and, using all his strength, swing her up onto the ice slab before it flattened her. And the third thing that happened was that the ice block itself, which had been sliding so quickly and noisily down the long, sloping cavern inside the hill, hit the stone wall end of the tunnel, **SMMASSSHEDD!** through the rock and shale with a dusty explosion, and flew out into the open air on the side of the mountain with Conor and Charlie on top!

The icy slab, no doubt having gotten used to the idea of sliding, kept on doing so. Charlie and Conor quietly gritted their teeth as they rode the glacial lump, both scared rigid and holding onto Conor's pickaxe for dear life.

And on it slid, as luck would have it, right the way down the southern path that Conor and Charlie had trudged up not half an hour before. The ice slid silently past the spot where Damian and Gulliver had goofed off to have their picnic, a discarded crisp packet and an empty bottle of blue ink the only evidence that they had been there. Conor tutt-tutted to himself; he hated people who littered, especially when they were scouts and should know better. But he hadn't much time to think that thought – the ice was moving too fast!

The slab was approaching the scouts' base camp now, and it was almost flying! The rain had stopped and the sun had come out, which was good news for the scouts in the camp, but less good news for the two friends who were riding a slippery block of ice down a steep slope at high speed. It picked up pace as it slipped right between two of the scout tents, dislodging a toe rope and causing one of the tents to collapse like a slowly deflating balloon. Conor was sure he saw the blue ink–stained face of Gulliver looking out of the crumpling tent's door flap. Swiftly and noiselessly the ice slid past the sleeping figure of scout leader Dennis Deegan, propped up in a foldable chair with his binoculars on his lap.

As much as they wanted to howl in terror, Conor and Charlie kept quiet. Although they had done nothing wrong really, they were sure that

Dennis, with his suspicious mind and mean outlook, wouldn't see it like that and would find some way of punishing them. Especially if he caught them riding a massive hunk of frozen water right through the scout camp at breakneck speed.

The ice slid on through the sloping field and through an open gateway, towards the lake.

'Conor,' said Charlie, who had opened her eyes for the first time since the slab burst out of the cave, 'em, you see that tree?'

'The one beside the lough?' replied Conor.

'Yup, that's the one. Is that an elm or an oak?'

'I'm not sure,' said Conor. 'It's hard to see at this distance.' He grimaced. 'But I think I'll be able to tell you for sure in about five seconds! Five, four, three, two –'

KER-ASSHHHH!!!

With a loud *ker-boom*, the huge block of ancient glacial ice hit the tree (which turned out to be an oak, incidentally). Conor and Charlie were thrown clear by the impact, landing in the soft grass and rushes at the water's edge. Snowflake-like crystals of smashed ice and wobbly edged oak leaves fell on their heads like a gentle rain.

'Charlie, are you okay?' asked Conor. He was a bit out of breath, but unharmed. That ride, as scary and potentially life-threatening as it was,

was most definitely the most exciting experience he had ever had; he actually felt like laughing.

'I'm fine, I think,' replied Charlie, and then she did laugh. Conor joined in, and they rolled in the soft grass at the side of Lough Dan, holding their tummies and howling with relief that they were both still alive!

They were guffawing so loudly that they didn't hear it at first: the low moaning sound that seemed to be coming from the other side of the broad trunk of the old oak tree. But as their laughter subsided, the noise began to register in their brains – a deep, rumbling, moaning, groaning sound that echoed slightly out across the lake water, bounced off the shallow waves and travelled back to their ears. An almost unearthly, gravelly noise that sounded like ancient iron doors being pushed open for the first time in centuries.

They looked at each other, their eyes wide. Then suddenly the groaning stopped, and there was a little coughing sound. *A-heh.* This tiny, almost dainty cough was followed by a massive, gigantic, gi-normous **SNEEZE!** The leaves on the oak tree (those that were left, following the collision) shook with the noise.

Conor and Charlie tiptoed to the tree and cautiously crept around its wide trunk.

They. Could. Not. Believe. Their. Eyes.

Sitting on the ground, amidst broken shards of primeval glacial ice, was the biggest, hairiest, most tough-looking man (at least, they thought it was a man) that either of them had ever seen. He blinked his deep-set blue eyes twice, then scratched his jutting forehead with one hand and wiped his huge, wide nose with the hairy wrist that was attached to the other, leaving silver, snotty streaks up his arm. He slowly turned his head towards the two friends and did the very last thing that either of them could have predicted: he smiled.

CHAPTER FOUR
WALK TALL

The caveman (well, thought Conor, what else *could* he be? They did find him in a cave, after all) reached out and grabbed his spear. Charlie jumped back a little in fright, but the recently defrosted cave dweller hugged the spear to his huge chest and shivered. He looked a bit blue.

'Oh,' said Charlie, 'the poor thing's freezing!' She took her rucksack off her back and produced a picnic blanket from it. 'This might warm him up a bit.'

She placed the blanket carefully around the caveman's shoulders, and he pulled it tight around him. He gazed at Charlie with what looked like gratitude, then he fixed his eyes on Conor and pointed to his mouth in short, urgent, jerking movements.

'W-w-what's the matter, fella?' asked Conor. He took half a step towards the hulking figure. 'Is it toothache? No?' Conor was close enough to look into the creature's mouth. 'Ugh! Morning breath!' Conor recoiled, holding his nose.

'Ogg,' said the caveman.

'Ogg? Is that your name?' The caveman kept pointing at his mouth.

'So not toothache. And I don't have any mouthwash for your breath. That's what six thousand years of not brushing your teeth will do to you. Of course! He must be hungry! He hasn't eaten for thousands of years!'

Conor and Charlie searched through their backpacks and found a couple of chocolate bars. Charlie held one out to Ogg, who took it daintily with his huge fingers and popped it into his mouth, wrapper and all. He chewed a couple of times and swallowed. Then he smiled. Conor thought it was a nice smile, mainly because it made Ogg look slightly less blood-curdlingly scary. Conor passed the other chocolate bar to Ogg, and he gobbled that one as well. He was looking less blue-ish and more human now in the sunlight. More human, that is, until he stood up.

With a creak and an *oof*, the giant caveman raised himself off the grass to his full height. He was MASSIVE! Conor thought he must be at least as tall as Hightop McArdle, the captain of the local basketball team, the Clobberstown Dunkers, and almost as wide.

'He's a big lad, isn't he?' said Charlie.

'Holy moley,' said Conor, 'he's HUGE.' He stuck out his hand towards Ogg. 'Well, Mr. Ogg, eh, welcome to Wicklow.' He frowned. 'I suppose when you were frozen in that glacier, it wasn't called Wicklow … You and your people probably had your own name for it. Don't know what it was. Probably Ugg-low or something. But. Doesn't matter. Hmm. I'm babbling. Charlie? Am I babbling?'

‘Yes, you’re babbling,’ replied Charlie. ‘First you won’t speak at all, then you meet Ogg and you won’t shut up. Here …’ She lifted Ogg’s free hand and placed it over Conor’s. ‘Shake hands, boys. I think the two of you are going to be great pals!’

Both smiling shyly, the boy scout and the caveman shook hands. Ogg smiled, showing big, white, slightly uneven teeth.

The sound of car horns came from the distance. Charlie looked at her watch. It was nearly three o’clock! The first parents were arriving to pick up their kids from the scout camp!

'We better go!' said Charlie, putting her rucksack on her back.

Conor repacked his rucksack slowly. 'We can't leave him,' he said. Ogg looked at both of them. Despite his gigantic size, the poor lunk looked as helpless as a small puppy.

'Of course we can't leave him,' said Charlie, 'but you'll have to bring him home. We have no room for him in our house, but there's plenty of room in yours, especially since …' She wanted to say 'since your dad left' but wasn't sure how Conor felt about it. It was hard to tell how he felt about anything at all when he never spoke.

Much to her relief, Conor broke in and saved her the embarrassment of saying the wrong thing. 'We have room alright, but Mum would go crazy. If he's coming to mine, we'll have to keep him a secret for now.'

'How will we do that?' asked Charlie, not unreasonably.

'We'll have to smuggle him into Mum's car,' said Conor.

'And how will we do that?' asked Charlie, still not unreasonably.

'Haven't a clue. We'll just have to wing it and hope for the best.'

Conor took Ogg's hand again and began to pull him towards the scout camp. There was one little problem: Ogg wasn't budging. As hard as Conor pulled, Ogg wouldn't move. Charlie even tried pushing him from behind, but still Ogg stayed, stuck in place, as solid and unmoving as a dolmen stone. Then Conor had an idea. He took a packet of salt &

vinegar crisps out of his rucksack and opened them. Standing in front of Ogg, Conor put a crisp into his own mouth and MMMMMMMMMed and OOOOOOHHHHHed and rubbed his tummy. These were *really* tasty crisps, and Conor wanted Ogg to know it.

Ogg licked his lips. He was still starving after his six-thousand-year fast, and those crisps smelt delicious.

Conor moved away from Ogg, into the woods on the path to the camp, dropping a salt & vinegar crisp on the ground every couple of metres. Ogg moved with him, stopping to gobble up a crisp from the trail that Conor was making and then moving on to the next, getting closer to the camp with each mouth-watering crunch. Charlie shook her head at Conor's ingenuity and quickly followed behind them.

As they neared the camp they could hear the chaos of all the kids rushing around, gathering up their equipment and stuffing it into the boots of their parents' cars. Through the trees at the edge of the camp, Conor could see his own mum, Clarissa, leaning on the bonnet of her car and looking at her watch. He looked into the crisp bag. There were three or four crisps left: just about enough for what he had in mind.

'Okay,' said Conor. 'Charlie, I need you to go up to my mum and ask her to help bringing my stuff out of the boys' tent. Tell her you're not allowed go in, and I am running an errand for Dennis Deegan. I'll use the last of the crisps to get Ogg over to the back of the car, and I'll get him inside. If we throw the picnic blanket over him, maybe Mum won't notice.'

'Lucky you have an estate car,' said Charlie. 'He will just about fit. You'll have to find an excuse to keep the windows open, though. Remember – this guy hasn't had a bath for six thousand years. Peeee-eeeewww.'

She laughed and ran off towards Clarissa. While Charlie was busy spoofing his mum, Conor led Ogg around to the back of the car, which was half hidden by trees from the rest of the camp. He opened the hatchback and threw in the last couple of crisps. Ogg scrambled in, eager to get his huge hands (and teeth) on the tasty treats. Once he was safely inside and happily munching, Conor covered him with Charlie's picnic blanket.

'Be quiet, Ogg. Understand?' said Conor, motioning with his finger to his lips. Ogg pulled the blanket over him, smiled at Conor, and looked like he was just about ready to fall asleep. Conor hoped he would. Then he hoped that if he did, he wouldn't snore. *Holy moley*, thought Conor. He had arrived at the scout camp with nothing but a beaten-up rucksack, and he was leaving with a fully grown, recently defrosted, six-thousand-year-old caveman. Funny how things work out.

The drive home was as frosty as the glacier Ogg had been stuck in. Conor's mum wasn't too happy at having to gather all Conor's belongings up, even though Charlie had helped her; she wasn't happy that they were practically the last to leave the camp because of 'stuck-up, nose-in-the-air, hoity toity' Dennis Deegan's last-minute (bogus) errands that Conor had to do; and she definitely wasn't happy that Conor insisted on having ALL the car windows open as they drove. He claimed it was because he had recently become allergic to the smell of the Christmas tree–shaped pine air freshener that hung from the rear-view mirror. Clarissa offered to chuck it out the window, but Conor wouldn't let her, telling her all about Gulliver and Damian's littering on the side of the mountain. So the windows stayed open; Ogg, hidden in the back, stayed asleep (thankfully not snoring); and Conor stayed talking – which Clarissa found odd, as he was usually much quieter. Maybe this scouting lark was good for him after all!

Their home was in Clobberstown, an area of South Dublin nestled in the foothills of the Dublin Mountains. It was famous for three things: stray horses on all its green areas, the Clobberstown Dunkers basketball team, and its proximity to a large shopping centre that was called the Square, even though it quite plainly had a pyramid on its roof.

The Corcoran house was a three-bedroom semi-detached building with a scraggy garden at the front and an even scraggier one at the back. Where the lawns should have been, there were just weeds – the grass seemed to be much more interested in growing up through the cracks in the concrete paths.

Clarissa pulled the car into the small driveway at the front of the house and switched off the engine. She had a thumping headache, probably the result of working four hours already today, even before she went to pick up Conor from deepest, darkest Wicklow. Since Conor's dad had walked out on them, Clarissa had worked four jobs just to make ends meet. It seemed to Conor that she was always working – during the week she was a part-time nurse in Shady Acres old people's home and a part-time hairdresser in Sherlock Combs hair salon, and in the evenings she worked part-time in a fish and chip shop called The Codfather. At weekends she manned the desk (or wo-manned the desk, to be more precise) in Clobberstown Leisure Centre, all day Saturday and 8am to 12 noon on Sundays. Sunday afternoon was her only time off and she usually spent it with her boyfriend, Frank, so she wasn't best pleased to have to spend *this* Sunday afternoon picking up her son from scouts.

'Come on, Conor,' she said, getting out of the car with a *humph*-ing sound. 'You'll have to bring in your stuff yourself. I'm going for a lie down – I've a steaming headache.'

Conor was relieved. He had spent the car journey home frantically trying to think of a plan to get Ogg out of the car boot and into the house without his mum noticing, so this maternal cranial cramp was perfectly timed.

When he was sure his mum was safely up the stairs and in bed, Conor took in his scout stuff from the back seat of the car and put it away neatly. Then he went back to the car and opened the hatchback boot, where he had left Ogg sleeping under the picnic blanket. It was empty! He ran around to the back seat, but there was no caveman sitting there either. A very strange feeling came over him. Had he *dreamed* he found a caveman? Just thinking about it now, standing outside his house in dear old Clobberstown, the whole idea of finding a live, six-thousand-year-old caveman frozen in a mini-glacier and hidden in a cave seemed sort of … well, far fetched?

Then he heard it. A deep, rumbling bass sound that shook the glass in the window panes slightly. It seemed to be coming from the side of the house. Conor peeked around the corner into the messy side passage. The path that SHOULD have led to the back garden was partially blocked with the rusty red skeletons of old, battered bikes, an overgrown creeper bush, and the big disused dog kennel. The DOG KENNEL! Conor trotted over and looked inside. There was Ogg, fast asleep, with the picnic blanket pulled over him. So, not a dream after all. The huge caveman cradled his wooden and stone spear like a teddy bear in his huge, hairy arms. Cobwebs inside the kennel shivered and shook as he snored his low snore.

The caveman must have somehow sensed Conor in the doorway of the kennel, because in his sleep, quite loudly and distinctly, he said, 'Con. Nor.'

Holy moley, thought Conor, *he knows my name!*

EXHIBIT 1
EXTRACT FROM OGG'S DIARY
OGG GETS FROZEN IN ICE

CHAPTER FIVE

OGG'S DUVET DAY

Conor woke the next morning to the sound of his alarm clock. When he sleepily opened his eyes, the first thing they focused on was an A4 refill pad page taped to the chair beside his bed. It read: 'NOT A DREAM!' His eyes sprung open. OGG!

He jumped out of bed and hastily pulled his trousers on over his pyjama bottoms. He ran down the stairs, two at a time, not worrying about the racket he was making as he knew his mum had already gone to work in the old people's home. She was always up and out a couple of hours before Conor, leaving him to fend for himself with breakfast and getting to school.

He opened the front door and looked around the side of the house. There was Ogg, sitting outside the kennel, scratching his matted, hairy head. He looked like he had just woken up too. Conor was glad that the thick creeper bush kept Ogg hidden from the view of anyone walking up Clobberstown Crescent.

Ogg looked up. 'Con! Nor!' he said and smiled a huge, toothy smile.

So it wasn't a fluke, thought Conor. He CAN speak. Well, kind of.

Ogg got to his feet, which were huge and just as hairy as his arms. Conor took him by the hand and led him into the house, after first checking that no passersby or nosy neighbours were looking.

Ogg was a bit reluctant to go through the door, but Conor tugged him through. He supposed Ogg probably found the dark, drafty kennel to be more cave-like that this nice, warm house.

'Right, Ogg,' said Conor, 'I have to go to school soon. You'll have to stay here until I figure out what to do with you.'

He led the caveman into the kitchen. Ogg was so tall he was practically hitting his head off the top of the door frames.

'Are you hungry?' Conor asked.

Ogg looked down at him impassively.

Conor pointed to his mouth and added, 'You know, hungry? Are you starvin' Marvin? Fancy a bit of brekkie?'

'Brekk. Eee,' said Ogg.

'That's the spirit!' cried Conor, amazed at how quickly Ogg was catching on to the language. Conor himself was almost three years old before he spoke his first word, and, being the quiet boy he is, he hadn't spoken that many since.

Conor looked through the kitchen presses. 'Okay, we have cornflakes, shredded wheat, Wheetie-Wheels?' He handed Ogg the packet of Wheetie-Wheels. Ogg shook it. He sniffed it. He stuck out his big tongue and licked it.

'No!' said Conor, remembering how Ogg had eaten the chocolate bars, wrappers included. 'You have to open the packet first!'

Ogg looked at Conor quizzically, then understanding seemed to dawn. He ripped the cardboard packet apart, and Wheetie-Wheels went flying all over the kitchen in a massive explosion of sugary toasted wheat.

Conor sighed. 'Never mind. Mum won't be back until tonight, so I'll clean it up later. How about we cook something?' He opened the fridge. 'We have sausages, rashers, fish fingers, a little bit of custard … Do you like eggs, Ogg?' He held up an egg to Ogg.

Ogg's face lit up. He held one finger up and put his other hand under the fur he was wearing and rummaged around. After a moment he took out of his furs the biggest egg Conor had ever seen – it was so enormous it made the egg Conor was holding look like a Tic Tac in comparison.

It was a greenish-blue colour and looked like it may have been laid by a prehistoric ostrich or emu. Ogg's hand, as colossal as it was, could barely hold it. 'Ogg. Egg. Ogg,' said Ogg.

Conor shook his head in wonder, shrugged his shoulders and took out the biggest frying pan he could find. Even that didn't seem big enough for Ogg's mega-egg, so Conor got up on a chair, climbed onto the kitchen worktop and reached up to take down the wok from the top of the press. His mum had bought it for cooking Chinese food, but she worked so much she never got time to cook any more.

Conor turned on the stove, heated some oil in the wok and, with Ogg's help, broke the heavy egg into it. The smell from the egg was ATROCIOUS! Conor had to take a kitchen chair and sit down! He pulled the neck of his school jumper over his face and opened up the window. He looked like a bandit from a cowboy movie, but at least it kept the stench out. Ogg looked delighted, standing over the wok as the egg cooked and licking his lips.

Conor wondered what a six-thousand-year-old egg would taste like and then decided he actually never wanted to find out.

When the egg was done, Conor had to use a garden spade to lift it out of the wok – none of the ordinary kitchen implements were big enough to shift it. He put it on a plate, and while he gathered up the huge bits of broken, jagged eggshell and put them in a bin bag, Ogg tucked in. He ate with no knife and fork, using only his bulky, sausage-like fingers. He smacked his lips as he ate, wiping his nose with his hairy forearm.

When he was finished, Ogg sat back happily in the chair and let out the loudest **BBuUuUuUuURRrRrRRPpPpPPP!** Conor had ever heard. He checked out the front window to make sure nobody else on the road had overheard Ogg's prodigious wind-breaking, but all out on Clobberstown Crescent – unlike in Conor's kitchen – was quiet.

Conor checked his watch. Time to go. 'Okay, Ogg,' he said, leading Ogg into the living room and sitting him down on the sofa, 'I have to go to school now. You will have to stay here until I get back.'

Ogg looked up at him from the sofa. 'BE GOOD,' said Conor. 'Don't answer the door. Don't answer the phone. Just sit here and watch the telly, and when I'm back I'll figure out what to do with you.'

Conor switched on the television, which came to life with colours and noises blaring. Ogg jumped up and hid behind the sofa. 'It's okay, it's okay,' said Conor. 'It's only morning TV, but I'm sure you'll find something you want to watch.'

He went into the kitchen and returned with the half empty, half torn apart packet of Wheetie-Wheels. 'Eat some of these if you get hungry again,' said Conor, and Ogg's head popped up slowly from behind the sofa. He could smell the Wheetie-Wheels.

As soon as Ogg was sitting back on the sofa with the Wheetie-Wheels packet in his lap, Conor grabbed his school bag and ran to the door. 'See you later, Ogg!' he whispered, not wanting the neighbours to hear. He closed the door quietly and set off for school, hoping that the six-thousand-year-old caveman he had left sitting on his couch wouldn't wreck his house.

Conor hadn't even reached his garden gate when his phone beeped. For one mad second he thought it was Ogg texting him, but he shook that crazy idea away – the caveman seemed to be very good at picking up words, but picking up a mobile phone and sending a text? Conor didn't think so.

He looked at his phone; it was from Charlie.

HOW IS R LITLE FREND? it read.

FINE, he texted back.

He was as economical with the written word as he was with the spoken word. Besides that, it is dangerous to text while you are walking down the street – you could be so distracted you could easily walk out under a bus.

Which is what Conor almost did. As he pressed SEND he stepped out onto the road, right into the path of a number 75 double decker. He felt a hand on his collar, and this time it was Charlie's turn to save HIS life. She pulled him back onto the path in the nick of time. The bus driver blew his horn and shook his fist.

'You shouldn't be texting while you're walking!' said Charlie.

'YOU shouldn't be texting ME while I'm walking!' said Conor. 'You should also learn how to spell!'

'I liked it better when you didn't talk so much,' said Charlie, with a laugh. 'Come on, the bell will be ringing in a couple of minutes.' They hurried off.

When they arrived at school, Damian Deegan and Gulliver Quinn were loitering at the front gates. Damian snickered a weasely laugh as Conor and Charlie passed through. 'Here comes Conor "No Mates"

Corcoran. Interesting fact: did you know, Gulliver, that Conor has to hang around with girls because no boys want to be friends with him?'

'I was not aware of that fact, Damian. That is indeed very interesting.' Gulliver did his 'griggling' thing again, grunting and giggling at the same time.

'Ignore them,' said Charlie, 'and don't take any notice of Gulliver. I think he's a bit worse for the ink.'

Gulliver put his hand over his blue-stained lips and looked guilty.

'Watch it, Charlie Finch,' said Damian, pushing himself off the wall he had been leaning on and blocking Charlie's way. He wagged a finger in her face. 'Just because you're a girl doesn't mean I won't fight you.'

Charlie narrowed her eyes at Damian.

'I mean, em, just because you're, em, a girl doesn't mean Gulliver won't fight you.'

'No, I won't,' said Gulliver quietly.

Charlie sighed and smiled sweetly. Then she grabbed Damian's finger and twisted his arm around his back. Damian made an AIEEEEEE! sound. 'Nobody, and I mean NOBODY, threatens to fight a girl. Do I make myself clear?'

Damian simply squeaked. Just then the bell rang. Charlie dropped Damian's finger, and he gasped in relief. 'Good! I'm glad we sorted that out!' said Charlie.

She smiled again and sauntered off to assembly in the school hall with Conor in tow. In tow of Charlie, and in AWE of her!

Ms. Hennigan, the school principal, took her place on the small platform at the top of the dingy hall. The hall was built in the 1970s and was in bad need of good repair. It had broken gym equipment around the walls and a rusty corrugated-iron roof, and it smelled faintly of the body odour of all the children who had trained there, played five-a-side there, put on plays there, and generally got sweaty there for the last forty years. Ms. Hennigan hadn't been there for forty years – she was relatively new to the post – but sometimes she felt as if she had been. Especially on Monday mornings. And even more especially on Monday mornings when it was raining – she could hear the first heavy drops beginning to hit the corrugated-iron roof. Oh no, that was all she needed.

She straightened her cardigan and called the school to attention. 'Welcome back, boys and girls. I hope you all had a good weekend and are nice and rested and ready for a fun week of work.'

What's fun about work?? thought half the school children.

'And I hope you remembered, boys and girls, that tomorrow is Bring Your Parent to School Day. I hope you have organised your mother or your father or your guardian to be ready to come in to the class and tell us all about what wonderful jobs they have – be they air traffic controllers, stockbrokers, landscape gardeners or homemakers. We look forward to hearing from them all.'

Damian, who was sitting in front of Conor in the hall, turned around to face him. After making sure that Charlie wasn't within earshot, he said snidely, 'What are YOU going to do tomorrow, Corcoran? You haven't GOT a dad, and your mum is never around.'

The rain was getting heavier on the corrugated roof, and poor Ms. Hennigan was having to speak louder to be heard. Some cold drips started to come down on the heads of the children and teachers through cracks and holes in the roof, and there were small cries of dismay from a couple of the kids. One teacher, who must have been a scout as a child, was prepared enough to bring an umbrella, which he popped open and sat under.

'Really, Ms. Hennigan,' whispered a small, mousey teacher with big teeth and bigger spectacles, 'when are we going to get that roof fixed?'

A drop of icy water splashed off her twitchy nose. This woman really looked like a mouse; all she was missing was a tail.

'As soon as we appoint a new caretaker,' said Ms. Hennigan. 'The last one, if you remember, Ms. Sniffles, was chased out of here by certain ruffian pupils.'

She glared pointedly at Damian and Gulliver, both of whom were snickering (again! Snickering seemed to be their favourite pastime. If there was an All-Ireland snickering team, Damian and Gulliver would be the captain and prop-forward) and picking their noses.

CHAPTER SIX
A DOG-GONE DILEMMA

After school, Conor and Charlie ran all the way back to Conor's house. They both had been thinking about Ogg all day and hadn't been able to concentrate on their school work at all. In art class, the students had to draw pictures of flying saucers to go with a story about aliens attacking Dublin, and Conor had drawn the spaceships as giant fried eggs flying over O'Connell Street!

They hoped that Ogg had sat there on the sofa, where Conor had left him, being good and watching TV. Some hope.

When they reached the house, Conor was alarmed to find that the front door was open. He ran inside looking for Ogg. He wasn't on the sofa in the living room, although the TV was still on.

'I'll check upstairs,' said Charlie and took the steps upwards two at a time.

Conor could hear her stomping about, going from room to room upstairs looking for Ogg while he did exactly the same thing downstairs, but the house was empty. There were no cavemen, frozen, defrosted or slightly chilly, to be seen anywhere.

Then Conor heard a cry from above. 'Smoke!' Charlie shouted. 'White smoke at the back window!'

They raced out into the backyard and sure enough, white smoke was billowing across the garden, past the huge old oak tree at the back wall. It seemed to be coming from the side passageway. The kennel!

As they thought, the smoke *was* coming from the dog kennel. Conor and Charlie bent down to peek through the doorway, their eyes watering with the thick white smoke. Ogg sat inside, warming his huge hands at a little fire he had built in the middle.

'He sure likes that kennel,' said Conor. 'You may as well stay here, Ogg. It doesn't really belong to anyone any more anyway. When dad left, he took the dog and left me.'

Ogg smiled. 'Dog. Gone. Ogg. Here.'

Charlie nearly jumped out of her socks! 'He can SPEAK?!'

'He must have picked it up from watching telly,' said Conor. 'I always told mum TV was educational.'

There wasn't much room for Conor and Charlie inside the kennel, so the two friends brought Ogg back inside the house. Conor looked at his watch. Good. Mum wouldn't be back until 11pm at the earliest. Plenty of time to spend with their new friend.

Conor and Charlie spent the afternoon showing Ogg all the wonders of modern technology. They showed him the toaster and how it toasted bread (although, for Ogg, bread itself was modern technology); they showed him the computer (Ogg tried to eat the mouse, but it was an ancient one with a lead attached, so they were able to pull it out of his mouth); and they showed him the gas fire, with the little switch to turn on the instant flame. Ogg was fascinated by this – his people had only just discovered fire themselves, and to have a wondrous device like this that produced a beautiful blue frame without all the fuss of dry twigs and bits of flint stone seemed like pure magic.

Just then the microwave oven that Charlie had been messing around with PINGGGed loudly and Ogg, deep in his gas-fire reverie, jumped up and ran out of the room. Not AGAIN, thought Conor as they looked for him in the living room, the bathroom and the little room under the stairs. How could a caveman the size of Ogg go missing twice in one day?

They eventually found him upstairs in Conor's bedroom, hiding on top of one of the wardrobes. 'I don't even want to know how he got up there,' said Charlie as Conor coaxed Ogg down.

Charlie checked the time on Conor's alarm clock; she had to go. She had to catch her dad before he went out to play Monday five-a-side at the leisure centre and remind him that tomorrow was Bring Your Parent to School Day.

Conor and Ogg saw her out. 'Seeya, Conor! Bye, Ogg!' Charlie chirped happily as she trotted down the path and up Clobberstown Crescent to her own house.

'Yep, seeya,' said Conor. He was still wondering what to do about Bring Your Parent to School Day. His mum was so busy working her four jobs that he didn't dare ask her to take time off to do it. And he couldn't ask her boyfriend, Frank Delaney, because, 1. He was a cop, and he would put the frighteners up half the class and most of the other parents who turned up – everybody has their guilty secrets, especially in Clobberstown, and 2. He was the most boooooring person that Conor had ever met. He even made being a police sergeant sound boring, with long, slow car chases pursuing some old lady on a walking frame who dropped litter in the street. The only time Frank's face lit up was when he talked about the mounds of paperwork that he and the other guards in the station had to do on a daily basis. Boy, did Frank like paperwork.

So, no, Frank wouldn't do either.

Conor rubbed his chin and looked at Ogg, standing in the hallway in his furs, with his long hair and big stone spear. A smile grew on Conor's face. He had an idea – it was a risky one, but it might just be crazy enough to actually work!

EXHIBIT 2
EXTRACT FROM OGG'S DIARY
OGG WATCHES TV

CHAPTER SEVEN
THE CAVEMAN FROM UNCLE

The next day was just as wet and windy. Conor got up early again and hustled Ogg in from the ex-dog's kennel where he insisted on sleeping.

'Right, Ogg, today is Bring Your Parent to School Day, and I'll be jiggered if I'm going to school without some kind of relation. So. Here's the plan. You're it.'

Conor fished around in his mum's wardrobe until he found what he was looking for: Frank's dungarees. Frank had worn them during the summer when he was painting the living room for Clarissa, and they were covered in paint splashes and globs of dried plaster. *Perfect*, thought Conor.

'I'm going to stick these on you, Ogg, and we'll see what you look like.'

This was easier said than done – Ogg had never worn clothes before, aside from his furs – but eventually, after much grunting and *oof*-ing from both parties, Conor managed to get the dungarees onto the oversized caveman, as well as a white tee shirt to cover his furs. Ogg looked almost human. Well, he was human. Mostly. He just looked more like a *modern* human.

'Stand up and let me see you,' said Conor.

Ogg stood up. The dungarees were big – Frank, like most law-enforcement officers, was a tall man – but they were nowhere near big enough for Ogg. The legs of the trouser part stopped just below Ogg's knees, leaving a length of hairy leg and two big, hairy feet on show. 'Hmm. We'll have to do something about that.'

Ten minutes later, Conor had cut the toes out of a pair of Frank's size-twelve runners that he found under the bed and jammed them onto Ogg's feet. He gave Ogg's hair a quick comb – well, a slow comb actually, it *was* quite matted – and HEY PRESTO! an instant relative. Ogg was still quite unshaven, and his hairy toes were sticking out of the front of each of the runners, but, Conor thought, he would have to do.

On the way out the front door, Conor had to send Ogg back inside with the flat-screen television set that he was trying to bring with him, tucked under his hairy arm. 'Ogg. Watch. Mammoth. Show.'

Conor sighed and held up the plug. It was only six feet long; the TV wouldn't even make it down the garden path, let alone all the way to school.

After pausing at the garden gate to make sure the coast was clear, Conor took Ogg's massive hand and led him down Clobberstown Crescent, before turning right onto Clobberstown View and down onto Clobberstown Main Street, past the bus stop, past the express supermarket and the post office, past the heavily graffitied children's playground and up the suitably named School Road, towards St. Gobnet's School. The rain was becoming heavy again, and the wind was howling through the trees, but Conor and Ogg walked on, hand in hand. Anyone who looked at them would have thought that the much bigger figure of Ogg was bringing his little boy for a walk, and not the other way around.

As they reached the school, Conor noticed all the different cars parked on the roads outside the gates. *Must be the parents*, he thought to himself. There was quite an array of automotive excellence on show, from sporty, expensive, two-door soft-tops to rusty old bangers with four doors but only one that actually opened.

With a deep breath, Conor led Ogg through the gates and into the school. They were both glad to get out of the storm. Here we go, Conor thought.

At his classroom door, the school principal, Ms. Hennigan, stood with a clipboard, ticking off each parent's name as they filed in. 'Ah,' she said as Conor approached, 'Conor Corcoran. And who is this, aheh, strapping young man you have brought along today?' She was giving Ogg a serious sideways glance.

'This is Ogg,' began Conor, 'I mean, this is my Ogg.' He gulped.

'I mean my, em, uncle … Ogg. Uncle Ogg!'

'Such an unusual name,' said Ms. Hennigan. She put out her hand, seemingly to touch Ogg's chest, but diverted at the last second and fixed the button on the strap of his dungarees instead.

'It's, em, short for Jim,' said Conor.

'Jim,' said Ms. Hennigan. She tried to write on the clipboard, but she hadn't clicked the button on her ballpoint pen. She looked up helplessly and gave a nervous laugh. Ogg smiled and Ms. Hennigan gulped audibly and staggered a little. *Grownups*, thought Conor.

At that moment Charlie stuck her head around the classroom door.

'Hiya, Conor, my dad's …' She stopped dead when she saw Ogg standing there with Ms. Hennigan.

'Ah, Charlie,' said Conor in a quiet voice, 'you know my Uncle Ogg … er, Jim?'

'Yes, of course, Uncle Jim. Come on in, Uncle Jim …' She led Conor and Ogg into the classroom. Ms. Hennigan stood staring after them, leaning slightly against the wall.

There was an audible GASP! in the packed classroom from kids and adults alike as Conor walked in with Ogg. Nobody had ever seen someone that tall. Or wide. Or, well, hairy.

Conor gave Charlie a small smile and went to his desk. 'What are you *doing?*' she whispered.

'I didn't want to arrive with no relation,' answered Conor. 'It'll be fine.'

Charlie snorted, 'Oh yeah, it'll be fine until Ogg has to speak!'

Now it was Conor's turn to gulp. He hadn't thought of that. Every parent or relation had to give a short speech on what they did for their job! What was Ogg going to say for HIS job? That he hunted woolly mammoths across the vast icy tundra of North Wicklow?? He couldn't even speak properly! *This is a disaster*, thought Conor. He sat down at his desk with his head in his hands. Ogg, standing by the wall with the other parents and relations, gave him a little wave.

One by one, the parents of the other children got up to speak. There were no air traffic controllers among them, but there were plenty of people who worked in supermarkets and in office jobs. There was even a lollipop lady called Sheila who brought in her giant lollipop to show the kids. (Her daughter Rebecca turned bright red.)

Then it was Dennis Deegan's turn to speak. As I mentioned earlier, Damian's father, as well as being a scout leader, was a high-flying, high-earning stockbroker, and he wanted everyone to know it. He smoothed down his orange hair, adjusted his gold cufflinks and smirked at the other parents as he took his place at the top of the class, as if to say 'all your jobs are rubbish compared to mine'.

Conor had heard this all before. Dennis regaled the scout troop regularly on how hard but how rewarding the world of stockbroking could be. So Conor looked out the window at the storm – it really was getting bad now, with lashing rain and winds that were making the weathervane on top of the school hall spin uncontrollably – then he put his head down on the desk and promptly fell asleep.

He only woke up when he heard the WOWs and JANEY MACKs from the kids around him as Dennis finished talking and handed them each a crisp fiver from his over-stuffed wallet. Charlie threw her eyes up in disgust but took the fiver anyway. Naturally, Dennis somehow 'forgot' to give Conor a fiver.

'Don't worry,' whispered Charlie, 'I'll split my money with you. Flash eejit – he doesn't know the value of it.'

Ms. Hennigan coughed. ‘Alright, settle down. Thank you, Mr. Deegan, for your most, eh, generous talk.’

Dennis smirked and flashed his too-white teeth to the class.

‘And now, we’ll hear from Conor Corcoran’s Uncle Ogg, I mean, Uncle Jim.’

All eyes turned to the massive, long-haired figure standing against the wall in too-short dungarees and shoes with the toes cut out of them. He looked back at them and blinked.

Conor sprang to his feet, thinking quickly. ‘I’m afraid my uncle can’t speak today because, well, he can’t speak.’ That much was true. ‘He can’t speak because he has, em, larry … um, larring ... eh …’

'Laryngitis?' said Ms. Hennigan helpfully. 'He's lost his voice? Ah, poor pet.' She shook her head and gazed at Ogg adoringly.

'That's it!' cried Conor. 'What SHE said! He's got larry-vitus, and he can't speak, so I'm going to speak for him.'

'This'll be a first,' muttered Damian Deegan to Gulliver. 'Corcoran never usually speaks either.'

Charlie turned around in her seat and glared at Damian, who shut up sharpish.

'You see, my uncle is a handyman. Which explains the handyman's clothes. Handily.' Conor took a deep breath and continued. 'He's great with his hands. He can fix anything – doors, windows, walls, toys, bikes, rocking horses, gutters, trampolines, garden sheds – you name it, he can fix it. He's Mister Fix It. Except his name is Ogg. I mean, Jim.' Conor gulped. 'And that's it. Thank you.' He sat down again and turned around to look at Ogg, who gave him another little wave.

There was a small clap from the class, who were slightly in bewilderment that Conor had spoken at all. But the applause, small as it was, was drowned out by a huge tearing, wrenching sound from down the corridor. Ms. Sniffles appeared in the doorway. 'Ms. Hennigan,' she shrieked above the noise, 'the school-hall roof, it's lifting off!'

Ms. Hennigan bustled down the corridor, followed by most of the parents and children. The double doors to the hall were wide open and through them they could see broad daylight as the corrugated-iron roof was raised, bent up at an angle by the high wind. Rain spattered down into the hall, covering the wooden floor.

'Oh, my!' cried Ms. Hennigan. 'Can anybody help?'

'Mr. Deegan is a scout leader,' shouted Charlie. 'I'm sure *he* can help!'

'Well, I …' stuttered Dennis Deegan, edging his way back though the crowd.

Suddenly the massive figure of Ogg made his way through the throng of people in the doorway. He walked over to the PE bars at the side of the hall and nimbly climbed up them, swinging off a rope attached to a ceiling cross-beam and flipping himself through the driving rain, up onto the roof. Ms. Hennigan gasped and clutched her chest.

Ogg took the loose panels of the rusty corrugated roof in his massive bare hands and, with brute strength, bent them back into place over the gaping hole. Hanging on despite the gale force wind, he produced a big wooden caveman club from

under his dungarees and battered and bashed the iron roof back into place.

The **clanging** and **kronching** sound inside the hall was very loud, but at least the rain wasn't coming in any more. The crowd cheered, Conor and Charlie cheering loudest.

Eventually Ogg, satisfied with his work, climbed back through a window high up in the wall of the hall and dropped down to the wooden floor. He was wet through.

The crowd of parents, relations and children gathered around him and clapped him on the back. They might have taken him up on their shoulders in celebration, but he looked much too heavy.

When the congratulations and the *well done, man*'s died down, Ms. Hennigan came up to him. 'So, Mr. Jim, I mean, Uncle Ogg. There's a caretaker job going here in the school. Starting tomorrow. If you're interested, that is, we'd love to have you?'

'Oh, call him Ogg, Ms. Hennigan, he actually prefers it. And he's interested in the job alright,' said Conor, quickly stepping between them. 'Uncle Ogg LOVES taking care of things.' *But*, he thought, *who's going to be taking care of Uncle Ogg?*

CHAPTER EIGHT
OGG JOB MAN

School ended early because of Bring Your Parent to School Day, and it was still raining heavily as Conor and Ogg made their way home to Clobberstown Crescent. Conor was so relieved that the day had gone well and so delighted with Ogg's new job that he didn't notice his mum's car parked in the driveway of their house. He and Ogg walked right into the kitchen, where Conor's mum was sitting. Luckily, she had a towel over her head and was face-down over a basin of steaming hot water, trying to breathe in the vapours. She couldn't see a thing.

'Is that you, Conor?' she said, muffled under the towel. 'Sorry, love, I'm choking with a cold. It's all this rainy weather.' She breathed in deeply. 'This is an old remedy that my mother gave me. You breathe in steam from boiling water and it soothes your lungs. I don't know if it's working, but at least my face is nice and warm.'

Conor motioned for Ogg to keep quiet. 'Hi Mum,' he said, shoving Ogg back out the kitchen door. 'I'm, em, just going upstairs to do my homework. See ya!'

He ushered Ogg out the door and into the dog kennel. Clarissa never went near the kennel – she missed her ex-dog too much.

'Mum. Sick?' asked Ogg when Conor had him safely inside the kennel.

'She just has a cold. She works too hard,' said Conor. 'You know, a cold.' He pretended to wipe his own nose and mimed a sneeze by way of explanation.

Ogg crawled out of the kennel and scampered around the back garden, gathering up weeds and leaves, seemingly at random.

'Get back in the kennel,' hissed Conor. 'Mum will see you.' But when he peeked through the kitchen window, Clarissa still had her head hidden under the towel.

Ogg brought the weeds back to the kennel and lit a small fire. He cooked up the leaves and weeds with water in a small pot he had taken from the kitchen, and soon the concoction was bubbling away, forming a greenish broth.

He gave the pot to Conor. 'Mum. Eat. Get better.'

Conor looked at the pot's soupy contents. It smelt okay, but he wasn't convinced.

'Mum. Eat. Get better,' repeated Ogg.

Conor took the broth into the kitchen, where his mother was still breathing in steam and coughing under the towel. 'I went to the health food store and got you some soup,' he said. 'If you want some, that is. If you're up to it.'

Clarissa was touched by her son's thoughtfulness. She emerged from under the towel, her hair wild and sticking up because of the steam. 'Conor Corcoran, I am amazed at how self-sufficient you've become. You are turning into a real little man.'

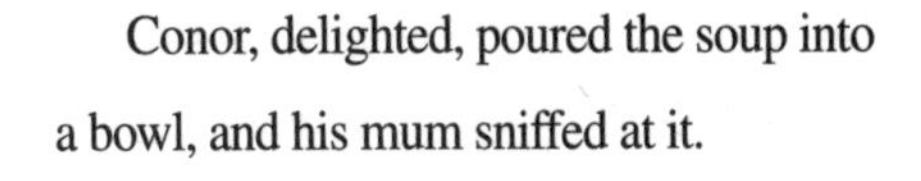

Conor, delighted, poured the soup into a bowl, and his mum sniffed at it.

'It smells nice, I think. My nose isn't working properly. What's in it?'

'This and that,' answered Conor truthfully. 'Mostly greens. It's good for you. So I hear.'

Clarissa stuck a spoon in and tasted the broth. 'Oh! It's an… unusual taste. But very nice!' She smiled up at Conor, 'Mmmmm, lovely.'

She was on her second spoonful and was about to ask Conor to pass the pepper when her head flopped down on the table, straight onto the rolled-up towel. She had passed out. Conor leapt to his feet, crying for Ogg, but Clarissa started to snore.

Ogg came into the kitchen and looked at the sleeping Clarissa. 'No worry, Conor. Mum better soon.' He lifted her up and carried her to the living room sofa to let her sleep.

When Conor came down the next morning, he found a breezy note from his mother waiting for him on the kitchen table, as well as a stack of pancakes and a jar of chocolate spread.

Ogg knocked at the kitchen window, and Conor let him in the back door. He was still wearing his handyman gear, which was just as well, as that morning was his first shift as caretaker for St. Gobnet's School.

Before they went to school (for Conor) and work (for Ogg), Conor made Ogg take a shower. Six thousand years frozen in ice kept Ogg fairly fresh, but everyone – even cavemen – needs a shower once in a while. Ogg was filled with wonder at the warm rain falling from the showerhead, and Conor ended up worrying about the water charges and hammering at the door to get him out.

When Ogg emerged, dressed as before in the workman dungarees, he looked much cleaner. His hair was less matted and was neatly brushed, and he had ditched some of his furs, which made him look trimmer and less bulky. He looked almost like a modern person, apart from his heavy forehead and unibrow.

When they arrived at the school, Ms. Hennigan immediately put Ogg to work, painting some tool sheds on the school allotment. Conor sniffed the air: he could have sworn Ms. Hennigan was wearing perfume.

Ogg wasn't used to holding a paintbrush – he normally did cave paintings with his fingers – but he soon got the knack of it, and, under the watchful (and admiring) eye of Ms. Hennigan, he finished the entire shed before little break.

'Very impressive,' said Ms. Hennigan, helping Ogg down from the ladder (not that he needed any help). 'I can see you're a dab hand with the paintbrush, unlike the last caretaker we had. Did you hear about him?'

Ogg shook his head. He had no idea who the last caretaker was. He hadn't even heard of paintbrushes until that morning.

'Wee Willie Whelan, his name was. An absolute disaster from start to finish. Do you know, one day last year, on the hottest day of the summer, I asked him to help put sunblock on the little ones. Do you know what he put on them? Vegetable oil. The poor children were running around the school yard with black smoke rising off their heads. Two of them caught fire!'

Ogg grunted.

'But you, Ogg,' cooed Ms. Hennigan, who, despite having helped Ogg off the ladder minutes ago still hadn't let go of his hand, 'you have the rough hands of a hard-working man, the hands of a warrior. But you also possess the gentle soul of a …'

But we will never know what it was that Ogg possessed the gentle soul of, because at that moment there came a loud, frightened cry from the field behind the allotment.

The fields around the school were used for grazing horses and animals, and this one was no different. It contained an animal, namely a bull. A very large, very angry bull with two sharp horns. The field also contained a small girl, namely Charlotte Finch, otherwise known to you and me as Charlie.

Charlie had gone into the field to gather conkers and horse chestnut leaves to draw in art class (like all the most intelligent, trustworthy and good-looking people in the world, she loved to draw), but unfortunately she had forgotten all about the bull. She noticed the aforementioned very large, very angry bull sitting in the corner of the field only after she had tramped halfway across it. She also noticed, for the first time, that the school jumper she was wearing was bright red. She wasn't sure if it was a myth that bulls hated the colour red. In fact, she was so scared at that moment that she couldn't actually remember whether or not bulls ate people.

The bull jumped to his feet and started running towards Charlie. Charlie started running away from the bull. She also started shouting, which is what alerted Ogg to her predicament.

‘Char. Leee,’ he said and dropped Ms. Hennigan’s hand. He leapt the fence into the far field and sprinted over the grass toward the bull. He clapped his huge hands and shouted to get the bull’s attention, and when the bull changed course to charge Ogg instead of Charlie, Ogg just stood dead still, waiting for him.

The bull charged forward at full speed, but when he reached Ogg, the caveman sidestepped him easily and grabbed onto one of his sharp horns. Using the bull’s own speed to power his leap, Ogg flipped himself over the dangerous set of horns and onto the bull’s back.

Once there, Ogg used his strength to pull back the horns, slowing the bull down to a canter, then a trot, a walk, and then to a full stop. The bull dropped down on the ground, exhausted, with Ogg still on top. Ogg leant down and whispered ancient words into the bull’s ear, and the huge animal closed its eyes and drifted off into a peaceful sleep.

Ogg looked up. Charlie had made it to the fence and was safe in Ms. Hennigan's arms.

'Oh, you silly girl!' cried Ms. Hennigan. 'My poor pet, are you alright?'

'Yes,' said Charlie, 'thanks to Ogg.'

'Yes, indeed,' cooed Ms. Hennigan. 'A man of few words, but many talents …'

EXHIBIT 3
EXTRACT FROM OGG'S DIARY
OGG, THE BULL WHISPERER

BULL!
CHARLEEE!
DANGER!
OK
SLEEPY BULL...
ZZZZZZZ
JOB DONE!

CHAPTER NINE

NO PLACE LIKE HOME

Two days later Conor and Charlie's class had a school trip to the Museum of Natural History in the centre of Dublin. Conor was one of the few kids in the class who was actually looking forward to it. Damian was one of the many who wasn't. 'Who wants to look at dusty old dead animals?' said Damian. 'If I wanted to see a bunch of oversized animals lying around and not doing much, I'd go to the next Clobberstown Dunkers match.'

Gulliver, as usual, griggled and took a sneaky swig of ink from the bottle he had hidden in his bag.

Ms. Hennigan came into the classroom. 'Alright, children, the bus is here but I'm afraid your class teacher isn't. Ms. Sniffles has called in sick, and we're short-staffed here, as you know, so I've asked our new caretaker, Mr. Ogg, to come with us to keep an eye on you.'

Conor and Charlie sat bolt upright and stared at each other. Ogg came into the classroom, ducking his head to pass under the doorframe. He smiled at Conor and Charlie and gave them a little wave. What was this? How could Ogg look after kids?? He could barely look after himself!

The children filed onto the bus, which was parked in the set-down zone at the front of the school. Ms. Hennigan fussed them along the aisles, clucking like a mother hen. She sat down in the seat beside the driver at the front of the bus and then noticed that Ogg hadn't boarded. She looked out the side window and saw Ogg standing at the door, staring wide-eyed at the steps. 'Come along, Mr. Ogg,' said Ms. Hennigan. 'We don't want to be late!'

Ogg was frozen to the spot, but this time it seemed like he was frozen with fear rather than ice!

Charlie stood up from her seat and trotted down the aisle to where Ms. Hennigan was sitting. 'I'm sorry, Ms. Hennigan,' she said. 'You see, Conor's uncle is a bit scared of buses, ever since …' She got stuck there. Why would anyone be scared of buses?

'Ever since he was bitten by one as a child!' piped up Conor, who had scuttled down behind Charlie. Charlie looked at Conor dumbfounded. Conor just shrugged.

'Oh, the poor pet,' said Ms. Hennigan, who, luckily for Conor, wasn't really listening to him. 'Scared of buses? Oh, my poor big brave caretaker.'

She was up from her seat and off the bus like a shot. She gently took Ogg by the hand and led him onto the bus. 'There we go, Mr. Ogg. If you're nervous or are prone to motion sickness, I'm happy to hold your hand the whole way into town.'

And she did, but she had to do it long distance, because Ogg was too big to sit in the single seat beside her and had to sit in the double seat opposite. With his other hand he gripped the handle on the side of his seat, his knuckles white. He kept his eyes tightly shut the whole way in.

Although the journey into the city was short enough, there was a school tradition of singing songs whenever they were on public transport. A few of the boys and girls took turns leading the rest of the class through rousing renditions of such classics as 'Nobody Likes Me, Everybody Hates Me, I'm Going Out to Eat Worms'; 'Oh, You're All Very Quiet at the Back'; and that all-time perennial favourite, 'Stop the Bus, I Want a Wee Wee'.

Conor and Charlie didn't join in – they were keeping an eye on Ogg and on Ms. Hennigan, who was patting and stroking his huge, hairy hand, making strange tut-tut noises and repeating the words 'poor pet, poor poor pet'.

When they arrived at the Natural History Museum, Ogg wrestled his hand from Ms. Hennigan's grip and was first off the bus. He stood like a sentry guard as the boys and girls got off.

'Well done, Ogg,' said Conor quietly and squeezed his arm. 'I'm proud of you.' Ogg smiled down at him.

Ms. Hennigan counted heads – they were all there. 'In we go,' she trilled and marched ahead through the impressive museum doors, with the children following and Ogg bringing up the rear.

As soon as they were inside, the kids scattered in all directions, but Ogg stood still as a standing stone in the foyer. His eyes bulged. All around him were animals and creatures he was very familiar with! To his right was a massive stag, to his left was an enormous bison, and right in front of him was the mighty skeleton of an ancient giant elk.

'Isn't she beautiful?' cooed Ms. Hennigan. 'This elk must have been a beautiful specimen in its day.'

'Elk,' said Ogg.

They moved on into the museum, following the children.

The boys and girls were running from one display case to the next, reading about the stuffed animals contained in each. The museum was a truly amazing place to visit: it had thousands of exhibits of animals, birds, fish and insects from Ireland and Europe, and from Africa, Asia and Australia – all jam-packed into a high-ceilinged Victorian warehouse that was built in the 1850s. The ground floor and second floor held mammals and fish, while two balcony tiers that clung to the side walls held the exhibits of birds and insects.

The centrepiece of the collection was the huge skeleton of a blue whale that hung from the ceiling. 'I'd love a closer look at that sucker,' said Damian Deegan to Gulliver, and they set out to climb the steps up to the next balcony. They were stopped by a security guard.

'Sorry, lads,' he said. 'The balcony levels are off limits to the public. Health and safety.'

'What about those guys? Why are they allowed up?' asked Damian, pointing to a group of men on the third-floor balcony, all of whom were wearing white coats and seemed to be carrying suitcases.

'Visiting professors from England,' came the reply. 'They're allowed up because they are clever people, which you and your friend here definitely aren't.'

Damian looked at Gulliver. His mouth was covered in ink stains, and he was picking his nose with a blue-coloured finger. Damian couldn't argue with the security man. Instead, he turned around and picked on Conor.

'Hey, Conor. Check out the Neanderthals,' he said with a mean tone in his voice, pointing at the huge display area behind them. It had half a caveman village inside – cavemen and women were cooking and relaxing and playing with cave-children beside a stone age hut. 'Remind you of Uncle Ogg much?'

Conor looked at the display. Ogg certainly resembled these guys, but he was a good bit taller. If he was a Neanderthal, he must have been the biggest one in the village. Conor was about to reply to Damian when he felt a hand on his shoulder. A large hand. He looked up to see Ogg staring at the caveman village as well. He seemed to have tears in his eyes.

Suddenly they heard a girl's frightened cry from the centre of the room. Ogg sprinted towards the noise, with Conor and Charlie following behind. Conor smiled when he saw what was going on – one of the kids from the class was lying on the ground under the enormous prehistoric moose, which had been stuffed in the act of rearing up on its hind legs. She was hamming up being scared while another kid was taking her photo with a camera phone.

Ogg, of course, had never seen a camera and thought the moose was somehow alive and attacking one of his children! He took a running leap onto the moose's back and produced his caveman club from under his workman's dungarees. He forced the stuffed moose onto its knees (badly bending its internal metal frame as he did so) and began to clobber it on the head and antlers. The kids scattered, forming a ring around him, and started to roar laughing. The security man ran towards the ruckus and, panicked, fell into a display of stuffed rabbits and hares.

'Mr. Ogg!' shouted Ms. Hennigan. 'Stop at once, you big, handsome brute!'

Damian and Gulliver rolled around on the floor, clutching their tummies and laughing. Conor covered his eyes.

'Oh well,' said Charlie. 'That's one less moose on the loose …'

High above on the third-level balcony, the little crowd of visiting professors had heard the commotion and were craning over the railings to see what was going on.

The tallest one – a skinny man with a bald head, bushy eyebrows and extremely hairy ears – stared down at Ogg, his eyes wide with astonishment. He turned to the three younger professors. 'This is what I have always dreamt of finding, ever since I was a boy,' he cried, his voice crackling with excitement. 'If I am not mistaken, and I rarely am, that creature below …'

'What – the one in the dungarees, Professor Griffin?' asked one of the other professors nervously.

'That creature below, the one in the dungarees,' continued the hairy-eared boffin, 'is … a CAVEMAN!'

EXTRACT FROM THE FIELD JOURNAL OF PROF. JASPER PONSONBY-SQUIBB

What ho! The name's Professor Jasper Ponsonby-Squibb, junior anthropologist at the jolly old Snetterton Museum of Natural History in Norwich, England, and I have been given the dubious honour of keeping up to date the field journal for this scientific expedition to deepest, darkest Hibernia. Or 'Dublin', as the natives would call it.

I've never kept a scientific field journal before, so apologies in advance if I lapse into what my lord and master, Professor Cromwell Griffin (also known as 'He Who Must Be Obeyed' or 'Old Bushy Ears'. Honestly! The amount of hair growing out of that crotchety old egghead's ears is nothing short of scandalous. It's also nothing short of five inches long, the dirty devil.) Anyway, where was I? Oh yes, apologies in advance if I lapse into what my lord and master, Old Bushy Ears (really! It's long enough for plaits!) would refer to as 'less than scientific terminology' in these pages, but it IS the first time I've been ordered to keep a field journal, and it's also the first time I've been to Ireland! In fact, it's the first time I've been outside Norwich, so I must admit to being super-excited!

So, back to the journal. Old Bushy Ears – I mean, the honourable and esteemed Professor Griffin – instructed me to record facts, so I shall now endeavour to do so.

Professor Griffin, under-professors Winston Bone and Gerard Flint and I arrived at Dublin Airport at 0715 this morning. After shaking hands with all the other passengers on the plane (some 127, as I recall) – an act of kinship with my new Irish brothers for which I received a severe verbal reprimand from Old Bushy Ears – we proceeded to the baggage carousel. A forty-five minute wait for our baggage ensued, which brought about much impatient huffing and puffing from He Who Must Be Obeyed. We then realised that we had only brought hand luggage. Twelve minutes later, when Old Bushy Ears had finished shouting at us, we set off for the taxi rank.

This was my first real taste of Ireland, as the taxi driver, a stocky, stout fellow with a twinkle in his eye, greeted us in the cherished language of his ancestors, the 'as Gaeilge'. He patted down his traditional Aran jumper over his sizable tummy, turned around in his seat and said in his lilting Irish brogue, 'Story, bud? Janey mack, itz brass munkees ou' dere, wha'? Youze from England, wha'? Where iz yiz goin'?'

A quick look in my Irish-English dictionary told me that he was commenting on the weather and requesting information on our intended destination. 'Good morning to you too, my good man! Yes, it IS unseasonably chilly for this time of year. We have just arrived from Norwich, and we wish to be taken to the Irish Museum of Natural History, if you please.'

Under-Profs Flint and Bone nodded furiously, and I fancy even Old Bushy Ears looked a little impressed with my grasp of the Irish language.

'No bodder, ladz,' said the cabbie. 'I'll have yiz dere in deh jiffy.'

Well, who knew that Dublin Airport was situated so far from Dublin City? All in all, the taxi journey took over SEVEN hours. Having said that, it WAS a charming trip, as we passed several famous Irish landmarks, such as the Rock of Cashel, Newgrange, Bunratty Castle and the Giant's Causeway, before finally reaching the city centre. All charming in the extreme, but one couldn't help wishing that the Irish had built Dublin Airport a little closer to Dublin itself.

On (finally) arriving in Dublin, and despite our protests, Professor Griffin insisted on us going directly to the Natural History Museum, where, after having a much needed tinkle (well, it WAS a very long taxi trip), we were shown around the exhibits by a jolly little security man. The museum turned out to be a lot larger than the one we have in jolly old Snetterton. We were on the third floor, which is a sort of balcony that goes around the top of the building, when we heard the most enormous kerfuffle from the public area below.

We all looked over the railing (apart from Bone, who is afraid of heights) and saw the most extraordinary sight – a very large man, who seemed to be with a very large group of very small children, had launched himself onto the back of a huge stuffed moose and wrestled it to the floor. He had a wooden club in his hand and was bonking the moose on the head with it. It was almost like he believed the moose to be alive!

Professor Griffin got very excited. There was something about the way this huge man attacked the moose, and something about his massive size and his hair and the cut of his jaw that made Old Bushy Ears convinced (against all reason, mind you!) that this behemoth of a man wasn't actually a man at all – Griffin believes he's a real, honest-to-goodness, genuine CAVEMAN!

Now, how that could be, I have no idea. And neither does Old Bushy Ears. But he has made it our mission over the next few days of our stay to PROVE that this person IS an actual caveman. The Professor wants to capture him so he can study his brain. I'm not certain, but I THINK I heard him use the word 'dissection'...

Oh, lordy. I think poor old Professor Griffin may be slightly off his rocker.

CHAPTER TEN
ALMOST A FAIR COP

After many apologies and assurances from Ms. Hennigan to the museum staff that nothing even remotely like the moose-battering incident would ever happen again, the bus eventually left for the return journey to Clobberstown. Ogg was quiet and subdued the whole way, and even the kids didn't really feel like singing, although they did do a solid fifteen minutes of 'Show Me the Way to Go Home' as soon as the bus left the city centre and got on the motorway.

Conor and Charlie walked with Ogg back towards Conor's house.

'You mustn't blame Ogg. It's his nature,' said Charlie, holding Ogg's hand. 'He just saw the moose attacking Sinead and assumed the worst.'

'I know, I know,' said Conor. 'The big lug will just have to be careful, or someone will realise he's a caveman.'

'Yes, well, cavemen are people too, you know,' said Charlie and gave Ogg's huge hand a squeeze. 'Don't call him a big lug, you'll hurt his feelings.'

'And speaking of big lugs,' said Conor, 'Frank is here!' He came to a dead stop – he had spotted his mum's boyfriend's car parked outside his house. 'You know, Mum's boy-FIEND. Ah no, I thought they'd split up!'

Charlie headed home and Conor quickly hid Ogg in the dog kennel. 'Sorry, Ogg. I don't know what Frank is doing here, but don't come out until he's gone.'

Conor came through the door, noisily jangling his keys. 'Ah, Frank!' he cried. 'So GOOD to see you!'

Frank didn't have to be a cop to be immediately suspicious – Conor was never that friendly to him. He smoothed down his moustache and coughed, raising himself off the sofa to his full beanpole height. He brushed dandruff off his police-uniform collar. 'Hello, young Conor.'

Why does he always call me 'young Conor', wondered Conor to himself. *Are there so many Conors in his life that he has to categorise me?*

'I, um, just called in today,' Frank continued, 'while your mum wasn't, um, here, to, um, ask you a question. You know, about your mum. Um. And me. You see …' He broke off mid-sentence. His keen policeman eyes had seen movement in the back garden. 'What? Who's that in the back garden, Conor? Is that one of your friends?'

He moved towards the back door in time to see someone ducking around the corner of the house. He opened the door and went out.

'Hello?' he called, and followed the mysterious figure around the corner.

Conor came after Frank. 'Frank,' he hissed, 'don't worry, I know who it is.'

'Well, who is it?' asked Frank.

'It's, em, it's …' Then Conor had a bolt of inspiration. 'It's a tramp! I found him on the green! He was nearly run over by some stray horses, so I told him he could sleep in the dog kennel. Just for tonight.'

'Those horses are a curse. Someone should do something,' said Frank, nimbly ignoring the fact that he was a policeman and that he probably should be the one who should be doing something. 'A tramp, you say.' He didn't sound convinced. He didn't look convinced either, for that matter, but, then again, he always had a suspicious look on his face – he was, after all, as I stated before, a cop. 'Well, it's very nice of you, Conor. But make sure he only stays one night. If he's still here tomorrow, I'll have to move him along. There's plenty of hostels in the city centre.'

'Don't worry, Frank, I'll make sure he's gone by tomorrow,' said Conor, and then to change the subject, 'Now, you said you had something to ask me?'

'Ah, um, yes. You see, me and Clarissa, I mean, me and your mum …'

Just then Frank's walkie-talkie police radio crackled, and a voice said something in cop-speak that only other cops could understand. CKKRZZ-CRK-UNIT-SEVEN-KRK-FRNK-TEWLPS-CLBBRSTWN-GREEN-AREA-RESPND? Or something like that.

'Frank Delaney responding,' said Frank into the radio and then, to Conor's relief, he headed for the door. 'Gotta go, compadre,' he said as he left. 'Antisocial pulling up of tulips on Clobberstown Green. We'll talk about your mum again, right?'

Conor nodded.

Frank turned at the gate. 'And remember what I said about that tramp. He's gotta go too.'

Conor closed the door and leaned against the wall in relief. He had gotten away with it.

CHAPTER ELEVEN
A LARK IN THE PARK

Conor, of course, didn't make sure that Ogg was gone by tomorrow. He didn't want Ogg to go, ever. Conor only had two friends, Charlie and Ogg, and he wanted to keep both, if that's alright with you, thank you very much.

He successfully hid Ogg from his mum all week long, and it was now Saturday – that meant it was time for another scout camp. This one was a survivalist weekend in the Phoenix Park. The Phoenix Park was a huge wooded area full of deer and wildlife that sat on the northside of the River Liffey, just outside the centre of Dublin. Despite its closeness to the city, the park had a kind of wild quality to it, not least because it was home to Dublin Zoo and the cries of the zoo animals could be heard throughout the park all night long.

Conor decided he couldn't leave Ogg behind at the house – Frank was already getting suspicious, and besides that, Ogg might get hungry and Conor didn't trust him with the toaster. There was nothing for it, Ogg would have to come.

That Saturday and Sunday, Conor's mum was working, as usual, in Clobberstown Leisure Centre. Her shift started at 8am, so Conor had plenty of time to get Ogg ready. After his mum had gone, Conor brought

Ogg into the house and let him have a shower. He went through Frank's clothes again and took out a pair of jeans and a big blue jumper for Ogg to put on. Along with the toeless runners, Conor thought Ogg looked alright – it was a nice change from the dungarees, at any rate.

Because Clarissa was working, Charlie's dad was picking Conor up. He wouldn't be expecting to see Ogg waiting for a lift too, but Conor thought he would give him the old 'it's-my-uncle-with-larry-gitis' line again. If it worked on Ms. Hennigan, the cleverest person Conor knew, it would work on anyone.

When the doorbell rang at 8.45am on the dot (Charlie's dad was a punctual sort), Ogg surprised Conor by trotting to the door and opening it himself with a cheery 'Morning!' for Charlie!

Holy moley, thought Conor, *Ogg's speech is getting better and better!*

Charlie laughed a pretty laugh and brought Ogg by the hand to her dad's car. 'This is Conor's uncle Ogg,' she told him. 'Is it okay if you give him a lift as well?'

'The more the merrier!' cried her dad.

Ogg got into the back seat, and the car immediately sank down almost to the tarmac on one side, its suspension under severe strain because of the massive weight. 'Ooh, big lad, isn't he?' said Charlie's dad, slightly worried for his vehicle's well-being. It was a bit of a banger, but it had been in the family for twenty-seven years now, and he loved it dearly.

'Dad!' whispered Charlie. 'Don't be rude!'

'Oops, sorry. Em, nice day, isn't it?' he said over his shoulder to Ogg.

'Morning,' said Ogg. It was a new word and he wanted to make the most of it.

Conor grinned at Ogg. He threw his bag in the boot of the car and they set off for the Phoenix Park.

As it turned out, Charlie's dad talked the whole way (politics, water charges, phone charges, TV talent shows – there was no subject he didn't know enough about to bore people silly with), so Conor didn't have to worry about Ogg's limited conversational abilities.

They arrived at the scout camp in the park and rolled to a stop beside where some scouts from Conor's troop were unpacking food and sleeping bags. Charlie's dad hopped out and took the rucksacks from the car boot.

Damian and Gulliver appeared when they saw Conor arrive, ready for a spot of early morning persecution, but they turned on their heels and walked off when Charlie and Ogg got out of the car. Ogg unfolded his huge frame to its full height as he got out, the tree branches far above the car's roof combing his long hair. He looked around and smiled. He recognised this place …

Damian's dad came over to them as Charlie's drove away. 'Ah,' said Dennis Deegan, 'I see you've brought your uncle with ye. Damian tells me it's Bogg, is that right?'

'His name's Ogg,' said Conor.

Ogg smiled and patted the bewildered stockbroker on the head. 'Eejit,' he said.

Conor and Charlie cracked up silently.

Dennis goggled at Ogg. Had he heard him right?

'Oooookay,' said Dennis. Then he shouted to the scouts, 'This weekend is all about survival, lads. And ye all know what that means: NO TENTS. Yep. Ye are all going to have to make your own shelters using nothing but natural materials. Now that Mr. Ogg is here, I think we'll split ye into two teams. I've a scout badge in advanced natural shelter making, so 'twill be no bother to me. Ogg, you can take the other team.'

He added under his breath (because he was afraid Ogg would hear), 'And *then* we'll see who the eejit is, heh?'

Some of the scouts were a bit nervous – they hadn't seen anyone as big as Ogg before – and opted to join Dennis's team, but Conor and Charlie grabbed their rucksacks and ran straight over to their caveman pal.

To Damian's disgust, Dennis ordered him to go with Ogg's group as well. 'To keep an oul' eye on him. Good lad, Damian, shoulders back.'

'One last thing,' said Dennis. 'After we spend the night out in the wilds, we will meet up again tomorrow on O'Connell Bridge in the centre of the city. And because this is a survival weekend, ye won't be getting taxis, cars or buses – no mechanical transport allowed. Ye'll have to hike it, walk it, run it, or, if you're feeling fruity, you could ride a horse.'

Damian smirked at Conor and Charlie. 'Should be no bother to you two at all. Sure isn't Clobberstown covered in piebald ponies?'

Charlie growled. Damian heard her and immediately ordered Gulliver to come with him for safety. Gulliver took a big gulp from his bottle of ink.

'Glurk. Such a filthy habit, Gulliver,' said Damian, hitting the nail on the head for once. 'I wish you'd give up drinking ink. It makes your teeth all blue.'

Gulliver smiled an apologetic, slightly blue-tinged smile.

Ogg shrugged his huge shoulders and marched his four scouts through the woods.

Charlie turned to Conor as they walked. 'If I didn't know better, I'd nearly say he knows where he's going!'

Now it was Conor's turn to shrug. 'Well, he's lived six thousand years longer than we have. You never know, maybe he used to visit the Phoenix Park thousands of years ago.'

Ogg led them far away from the paths, to a clearing surrounded by high oak trees. Although they were in a park that was visited by hundreds of thousands of Dubliners and tourists every year, when the scouts looked around the clearing they felt as if they were the first humans in history to have stood there. The grass beneath their feet was soft and long, the oak branches above swayed in a gentle breeze. It was absolutely silent; they couldn't hear people or traffic, even though they knew they were only a couple of hundred metres from the busy roads of Chapelizod and Strawberry Beds. Even Damian looked impressed. 'Janey mack,' he said, 'this place is actually quite nice.'

'Home,' whispered Ogg.

Conor, Charlie, Damian and Gulliver started to gather materials to build their shelters. They had read the scout manuals and had a fair idea what to do. Damian, being the scout leader's son, tried to take charge, but Conor and Charlie (and even Gulliver) ignored him and went off into the woods to find fallen branches and logs.

They returned after half an hour to an amazing sight. While they were gone, Ogg had built the most awesome shelter in the centre of the clearing. He had dug a small pit for the inside of the shelter and lined the floor with leaves, then, using branches and vines, he had constructed an eight-foot-high teepee. The outer walls were covered in ferns and, from an opening in the back, a ladder made of straight branches tied together led up to a lookout post high in one of the oak trees.

Ogg pointed up to the crow's nest he had made. 'For hunt elk!'

The whole troop laughed and followed Ogg into their cozy, warm shelter.

CHAPTER TWELVE
LET'S BE FRANK

As Ogg and his scouts settled into their camp that evening, over at Conor's house, the spare key rattled in the front door and Frank let himself in. He wasn't happy about Conor 'adopting' a random hobo. To tell the truth, though, he hadn't even mentioned it to Clarissa. Even though he was a cop and was meant to be rough and tough, Frank was slightly scared of Conor's mum. She worked quite a lot and was often very tired and very cranky. And everyone knows tired and cranky beats rough and tough any day of the week.

Frank opened the back door and went around the side of the house. He pulled the creeper plant out of the way and rapped on the roof of the kennel. Nobody home?

He leant down and stuck his head in the doorway of Clarissa's ex-dog's former digs, but no-one, vagabond or vagrant, was to be seen. In fact, he couldn't see much at all, it was so dark in there. But cops, like scouts, are always prepared. Frank took a slim flashlight out of his trousers pocket, clicked it on and climbed into the big kennel.

All over the floor of the doghouse were sharp stones. He picked one up. It looked like flint – is that what you call it? The stones were chipped into sharp shapes, kind of like arrowheads or axe blades, he thought.

And what was this one? He picked up another stone. It seemed to be carved into the shape of a dog. Or maybe a wolf, since it had pointy ears.

Frank swung his torch around the walls of the kennel. There were pictures on all of them, drawn on with charcoal from burnt bits of wood or sticks. There was a woman in one of them, and what looked like a couple of children in another – maybe a boy and a girl (it was hard to tell, as both the woman and the children had the same long hair and single eyebrow). On the third wall was a drawing of a wolf, the exact same as the carved stone Frank had found on the floor.

He looked at the carving of the wolf in his hand, and his cop senses started to tingle. Could this stuff be stolen property? *Hmmm.*

Frank took out his phone and searched for the number of the Natural History Museum. If this stuff – the flint arrowheads, the axe blades, the wolf carving – WAS stolen, the museum might have reported it.

The phone rang once, twice, three times. On the third ring someone picked up. 'Hello, Dublin Museum of – oh, I don't know, Natural History, I suppose? Professor Cromwell Griffin speaking.'

'Hi,' Frank said, 'this is Sergeant Frank Delaney from Clobberstown Station. I'm just wondering if you had any artifacts stolen recently. I've found some here – they appear to be Stone Age tools and stuff, but the strange thing is, they look quite new.'

'Don't you know how late it is? Hold on, did you say they look new?' said the voice at the other end of the line excitedly. 'Stone Age tools that look NEW??'

'Yes,' said Frank. 'No wear and tear. They look like they were just made yesterday.'

'It's a little late now, Sergeant, but myself and my team will be with you first thing in the morning,' said Professor Griffin, smiling a sneering smile. 'Now, tell me your address ...'

CHAPTER THIRTEEN

HOME SWEET CAVE

The next morning Conor, Charlie, Damian and Gulliver woke to a delicious cooking smell wafting in through the doorway of the teepee. They got out of their sleeping bags, rubbing their eyes. Conor sniffed the air. He couldn't quite place the smell, but he was glad it was a cooking smell he was smelling and not one of Gulliver's guffs.

The kids looked out the opening. Ogg was outside, and on the ground in front of him were huge leaves filled with raspberries, strawberries and nuts. He had built a fire and was roasting a rabbit on a spit over the flames. It smelt LUSCIOUS! The four scouts, still in their pyjamas, emerged from the makeshift teepee, drooling.

'I have to hand it to him,' said Damian to Conor, 'your Uncle Ogg is quite the cook.'

'Yes, he seems to be,' said Conor, wondering how early Ogg had gotten up to do all this foraging for food.

'Sit,' said Ogg. 'Conor, Charlie, friends, sit down. Eat.'

They sat down around the fire and Ogg handed them leaves filled with nuts, berries and succulent pieces of roast rabbit, which they ate with gusto. (Up until that moment Gulliver always believed that 'gusto' was his third cousin on his mother's side.)

Ogg gave Gulliver a plastic glass filled with fresh, crystal-clear stream water flavoured with honey. As soon as he tasted the delicious concoction, Gulliver licked his lips, quietly took the bottle of blue ink out of his pocket and poured it out onto the grass. He would never drink ink again!

When they had all finished, Damian and Gulliver were so impressed by the early morning feast that they actually volunteered to clean up.

'You know what,' said Damian to Gulliver, 'don't tell my dad, but that was the best breakfast I've ever had on a scout trip. I'm glad we went with Ogg, even though he IS a big lug.'

Gulliver frowned and smiled at the same time – a 'smrown', if you will. 'Hmm. Nothing wrong with being a big lug …' he said quietly.

Ogg turned to Conor and Charlie. 'Conor, Charlie,' he said, 'you come with Ogg.'

Ogg walked off through the trees. Conor and Charlie looked at each other and then followed him. They walked down a shallow, rocky slope to where Ogg was standing by a large, flat boulder. He had moved the rock to one side – there were scrapes in the earth and grass where he had shifted it. It was only a small rock, but it must have taken great strength to move it at all, Conor thought as he looked up at his enormous caveman friend.

Behind the rock was a smallish tunnel, just large enough for a sizeable man, or maybe even a caveman, to squeeze through. Ogg got down on his hands and knees and started to crawl into the passage. 'You come! Follow me!'

He wriggled in until all they could see were his big, hairy feet. They got down on all fours and followed him into the stoney burrow that went deep into the slope.

When they got to the end of the tunnel it opened out into a rocky chamber. Ogg certainly had been busy that morning – he had made torches from branches and had them dotted around the inside of the cave, lighting it up. 'Welcome,' said Ogg. 'Wipe feet.'

They looked around. At the side of the cave were long slabs of rock that looked like beds or seats, and in the centre was what looked like a stone table with four stone stools around it.

Charlie gasped. 'The walls,' she whispered to Conor. 'Look at the walls!'

The walls were covered in beautiful cave paintings. There were hunting scenes, with stick-figure cavemen throwing spears at mammoths and elk. There were scenes of cavemen building teepee shelters under grey clouds that were showering them with snow. There were also paintings of a woman with long hair and a unibrow, and two smaller cave-people, a boy and a girl. The boy was petting a wolf.

On the back wall behind the stone table there was a painting of a man who looked very like Ogg. 'My … family,' he said softly.

Behind them, unnoticed by Conor, Charlie or Ogg, Damian and Gulliver were looking around the side of the tunnel wall, their eyes wide with wonder.

EXHIBIT 4
EXTRACT FROM OGG'S DIARY
OGG GOES HUNTING
Ogg hunt now. Goodbye family.
Who is good boy? Wolfie is good boy!
Mammoth! Nom nom nom!
Family like elk burgers!
Home soon, Wolfie.
Is... Cold... Huh..?

RAWR!
What the..?
Wolfie is no mammoth snack!
SPLASH!
TRIP
Urk! Freezing!
Oh well, ogg better get used to cold...

CHAPTER FOURTEEN

THE OBNOXIOUS ANTHROPOLOGIST

'Ah, helloooo,' said Professor Cromwell Griffin as Frank opened the door. 'You must be Sergeant Delaney.'

'That's me,' said Frank, looking the anthropologist up and down with his cop's eye. He looked harmless enough, thought Frank, with his big baldy head and wispy grey hair, but what was up with those hairy ears? It was like the professor was trying to smuggle furry gerbils in his ear-holes.

Professor Griffin motioned to his team, who were standing behind him. 'Allow me to introduce my associates – under-professors Winston Bone and Gerard Flint, and that small fellow on the end is Ponsonby-Squibb. He's a professor too, if you can believe it.'

The tiny professor at the back shifted his feet in embarrassment and looked at the ground.

At that moment, Clarissa's car pulled up outside the front gate, and a very tired, very cranky looking woman opened the door, pulled herself out and stomped up the garden path with her head down. Her hair was wild and pulled over to one side in a slightly messy version of her usual bun, and she was wearing a light-blue nurse's uniform. In her right hand she was carrying a pair of false teeth. 'Ah no,' she said, looking at her hand, 'I'm after bringing home Mrs. Wilson's dentures again.'

She looked up and noticed the four white-coated professors for the first time. 'Who are these eejits?' she said to Frank. She was clearly in no mood to be trifled with.

'Professors from the Natural History Museum,' said Frank. 'What are you doing home so early, love?'

'Don't try to change the subject,' growled Clarissa. 'What do they want?'

Frank gulped. 'They're, em, here about the stolen Stone Age thingymajigs. The ones Conor's tramp was hiding in the dog's kennel.'

'WHAT??' said Conor's mum.

Frank gulped again. 'I was going to tell you …' he said weakly.

'Excuse me, madam,' said Professor Griffin, 'but it is very important that we establish the whereabouts of your son.'

'What do you want with Conor? Are you saying he's done something wrong?' said Clarissa, turning on the professor. Conor was her only son, and she didn't like the idea of this jumped-up, hairy-eared, baldy egghead accusing him of some sort of crime.

'Oh, he's fine, young lady, but he may be in trouble. That tramp he is associating with may not be all that he seems.' Griffin squinted at Clarissa and bent down so his face (and his hairy ears) was uncomfortably close to hers. 'That *tramp* may be an escaped convict. He may be a dangerous criminal.'

'Ah here,' said Frank, 'there's no dangerous escaped convicts on the loose. I'm a cop, I would have heard.' He put an arm around Clarissa. 'Don't be frightening her.'

'He's on a scout camp in the Phoenix Park,' said Clarissa.

'Thank you very much,' said Griffin, and he marched off with the three other professors in tow. 'You see, boys,' he said to them, loud enough for Frank and Clarissa to hear, 'treat the peasants nicely and they'll give you what you want.'

'I shouldn't have told them where Conor was, should I?' said Clarissa to Frank. She looked worried. And very tired.

'Probably not,' said Frank. 'Come on, we'll go and get Conor ourselves before those eejits do.'

EXTRACT FROM THE FIELD JOURNAL OF PROF. JASPER PONSONBY-SQUIBB

Well, that was a fine how-do-you-do.

The night before, when he had gotten the call, Old Bushy Ears became somewhat, well, animated.

'I've got him, lads! I've got him!' he was shouting while dancing around like he'd just been awarded first prize in a Crazy Professor competition.

Flint, Bone and I hadn't a clue what he was talking about or what he was so excited about getting. Flint suggested fleas, but Bone pointed out that he was dancing, not scratching.

This morning though, it all became clear to us – Griffin danced around once again, this time as soon as we left Clarissa's house.

'The caveman!' he chirped. 'I know where he is! He's camping in the Phoenix Park with some idiot child!'

My colleagues and I looked at each other. Now it was time to scratch OUR heads. 'The Phoenix what?' asked Flint.

'Park! The Phoenix PARK, you imbecile!' shouted Griffin, who had stopped dancing and took out his mobile phone. 'Hello? Directory Enquiries?' he said. 'I'm looking for the number of a helicopter rental company, please.'

Old Bushy Ears

He covered the mouthpiece of the phone with his hand. 'Gentlemen,' he said, 'if we are to catch a caveman, we have to out-think him - we must use every device that modern technology has to offer!'

Yes, but renting a helicopter? To chase down a possibly non-existant caveman?

I'm not sure the jolly old Snetterton Museum of Natural History will pay the bill for THIS craziness! I mean to say, cavemen? In modern-day Dublin??

I am now thoroughly convinced that poor Old Bushy Ears has gone as nutty as a fruitcake.

CHAPTER FIFTEEN
ROW, ROW, ROW YOUR LOG...

Ogg's scout troop packed their belongings in their rucksacks and cleaned up the camp, taking down the teepee and tidying up the leaves and branches. Unusually for Damian and Gulliver, they did their fair share of tidying, giving Ogg many curious glances as they did so. When they were all finished, the clearing looked exactly as it had done when they arrived the day before.

'Good,' said Ogg. 'Now come. We go O'Connell.' He was wearing his Stone Age fur coat over the blue jumper Conor had given him, and he was smiling to himself.

The four scouts followed Ogg through the trees, across the playing fields of an old secondary school and out onto the banks of the River Liffey.

'So, what are we going to do now, Ogg?' asked Charlie. 'Walk by the river all the way into the city as far as O'Connell Bridge?'

'No walk,' said Ogg. 'We swim like duck.'

'SWIM?' said Damian. 'You've got to be as crumbly as a pack of crackers. I'm not swimming all the way into town.'

'You can't swim anyway,' said Gulliver.

'Shaddap, Gulliver,' snapped Damian. 'I liked you better when you were drinking ink.'

'We not swim like this …' Ogg waved his arms in what looked like a passable butterfly stroke. 'We swim in … canoe!' He moved apart the rushes that were growing at the water's edge to reveal a wooden canoe that he had carved out of a big wooden tree trunk.

'Ogg, that is amazing!' cried Conor.

'There's oars and everything,' said Charlie, jumping into the canoe. 'Come on, boys, don't be scared. Get in, it's perfectly safe!'

The others weren't convinced, but, somewhat scared to disobey Charlie, they carefully boarded the carved wooden boat. It rocked a bit, but looked seaworthy enough.

Ogg got in last and sat at the back of the canoe. He took the oars in his huge hands and started to paddle off downstream, towards the city. The scouts sat back in the boat and relaxed. They looked up at the beautiful blue sky. This was the life!

They had almost reached the town of Chapelizod when they heard it – a sort of pulsing mechanical fluttering sound, low and steady, like the blades of a windmill on a very blowy day. It seemed to be getting closer.

Charlie pointed up into the blue sky. 'There!' she cried. 'That spot! Behind the trees!'

'I think it's a helicopter,' said Damian.

Ogg put down the oars and looked up towards the shape in the sky, shading his eyes from the sun. Gulliver took out his binoculars from his rucksack and squinted into the eyepieces. 'It IS a helicopter, and there are four people in it – all wearing white coats.' He dropped the binoculars. 'And one of them is holding a net!'

'Four guys in white coats with a net?' wondered Conor.

'Give me a look,' said Damian, grabbing the binoculars from Gulliver. The helicopter was coming closer now. 'Hold on a cotton-pickin' minute,' said Damian. 'I recognise these guys! They're visiting professors! I saw them at the Natural History Museum!'

'The museum?' said Conor. 'Ogg! THE NET! These jokers must be coming for Ogg! THEY MUST WANT TO CAPTURE HIM FOR THEIR MUSEUM!'

Charlie gasped. 'Quick, Ogg!' she shouted. 'We've got to get away from them! Paddle as fast as you can!'

Ogg started to paddle, his huge, muscled arms flexing as they moved the oars back and forth. The scouts joined in, helping him shift the oars.

As they started to glide through the water at a fair old speed, Damian shouted back to Conor, 'What is going on here, Corcoran? Why are these museum geeks chasing your uncle?' He couldn't hide the fear in his voice.

Conor took a deep breath. He had some explaining to do.

'Okay,' said Conor, 'long story short – Ogg is a caveman that Charlie and I found frozen in a glacier in the Wicklow Mountains. Those ancro–, andro–'

'Anthropologists,' chipped in Ogg, helpfully.

'… scientists probably want to capture him and put him in a weird zoo or something. Ogg is our friend and we're not going to let that happen.'

Damian and Gulliver glanced at each other. 'Fair enough,' shrugged Gulliver.

‘We kind of guessed that anyway,’ said Damian. ‘Gully, let’s get rowing.’ And they did.

The helicopter was almost overhead as the wooden canoe splashed down the weir at Chapelizod. There was a drop of a couple of metres and they almost turned over, but Ogg leaned his considerable weight to the left-hand side and the boat, with the four frightened scouts inside, quickly righted itself and sailed on.

The scouts could plainly see the four professors looking out of the helicopter windows; one of them was in the pilot’s seat. The craft hovered over the boat, keeping pace with it. The downdraft from the helicopter rotors churned the water and rocked the little boat violently from side to side. The scouts clung on while Ogg pulled on the oars.

‘Watch out!’ yelled Charlie.

One of the professors, a lanky one with a bald head and (even from this distance, Charlie could see quite clearly) very hairy ears launched a net downwards towards the boat. At that moment the canoe slipped under Chapelizod Bridge, and the net landed harmlessly on the roof of a passing rubbish lorry that was driving over it.

The canoe came out the other side of the bridge, and Ogg rowed harder than ever. The boat skipped over the water, heading downstream towards the city.

As they reached the city quays with the helicopter still in hot pursuit, Conor thought he heard someone calling his name. But how could that be?

They were in the middle of the river, rowing for dear life while being pursued by an extremely noisy helicopter! Nevertheless, he was sure he could hear someone calling him. He looked around, and on the south bank of the river he saw a small figure waving her arms and shouting. It was his mum!

'COOOONNNNNOOOORRRRRRRR!' she roared, hanging over the quay wall.

Frank had pulled up sharply on a one-way road at the side of the river when Clarissa, alerted by the hovering helicopter, had spotted the boat furiously being rowed down the river. Cars stuck behind him were blowing their horns and drivers were shouting out their windows at Frank, calling him a variety of most unpleasant names.

Frank hopped out and flashed his police badge. 'Move around – Garda business!' he said loudly. The drivers shut up and moved meekly around his parked car.

Frank joined Clarissa at the wall. 'Is that Conor?' he asked.

'He's fine!' said Clarissa. 'Charlie and another couple of boys are with him, but they're being chased by that helicopter! The big man in the boat is trying to save them!'

She started to dial 999, wondering which service she should ask for in the case of a child in the company of a large man wearing furs being chased downriver in a rickety wooden canoe by a helicopter full of men in white coats, when Frank took the phone out of her hands.

'Clobberstown Station, now!' he shouted, then, 'Seamus? It's Frank. I need a favour.'

CHAPTER SIXTEEN
BRIDGE OVER TROUBLED WATER

The small wooden log canoe skipped along the water, under Queen Street Bridge, Millennium Bridge and the Ha'penny Bridge, all the time with the helicopter following, just metres above, rising sharply upwards over each bridge and swooping downwards at the other side.

Inside the helicopter, Professor Jasper Ponsonby-Squibb was shouting to be heard over the noise of the rotors. 'Sir!' he cried. 'Professor Griffin! This is madness! We can't chase a boat in a helicopter like this! They are only children – they'll fall in the water and catch pneumonia and it will all be our fault!'

'Shut up, Ponsonby-Squibb! This will be the most important anthropological discovery of our age! He's a real live CAVEMAN! I'm going to be the most famous professor of anthropology in the world! I'm going to be rich! I should have known you wouldn't have the stomach for the chase – not like Flint and Bone here!'

'Actually, Professor,' said Gerard Bone, 'I don't think this is a particularly good idea either – Professor Flint only has a learner helicopter pilot licence!'

With that, Ponsonby-Squibb snapped. He lunged over the pilot's seat to wrestle the control stick from Flint's hands. The helicopter banked sharply to one side, and the rotors made a horrendous JUDDERing noise.

'That's it, Flint!' cried Griffin, hanging out of the window. 'Put her down! They are going under that wide bridge ahead. Land on it and we'll catch them at the other side!'

Flint didn't have much of a choice but to land. The rotors were catching and stalling, SHUDDERing to a stop and starting up again.

'Land on the bridge?' shouted Flint over the ear-bending sound of the failing helicopter rotors. 'We'll be lucky not to crash into it!'

Ogg's boat slipped quietly through the river water and under the bridge as the helicopter lurched out of the sky and dropped straight down for the last couple of meters, plopping with a massive **KKRRUUNNCHH!** onto the surface of O'Connell Street Bridge.

The professors emerged from the slightly wrecked aircraft, and Professor Griffin ran to the opposite side. 'Come on, you fools! What are you waiting for, the green man?' he shouted angrily. 'It's Sunday, there's no traffic.'

The three under-anthropologists reluctantly followed him over to the side of the bridge.

'Now,' said Griffin, 'we wait for the boat to come out, and then, by Jingo, we'll have 'em!'

They waited. And waited.

No boat emerged.

Griffin was bewildered. Where was his caveman?

'Flint, Bone,' he said, 'grab hold of Ponsonby-Squibb's ankles and dangle him over the side of the bridge. I want to see what's going on under there.'

Ponsonby-Squibb had started to protest when the little wooden log canoe glided out from under the bridge – completely empty!

'My caveman!' cried Griffin. 'Where is he? WHAT HAPPENED TO MY CAVEMAN??!!'

'FREEZE!' shouted Frank. He was standing on the bridge holding out his police badge, with Conor's mum behind him. Also behind him were twenty-four members of the Garda Síochána and seven Garda cars with their sirens on and lights blazing.

'WHERE'S MY SON?' shouted Clarissa, grabbing Griffin by the collar of his white coat.

He gulped. She looked even more tired and cranky than she had that morning in Clobberstown Crescent – and she had looked pretty tired and cranky then. Griffin just pointed at the empty boat, floating downriver towards Dublin Bay.

'I'm so sorry, we tried to stop him,' said Ponsonby-Squibb meekly. He was trying his best to put the 'apology' into 'anthropology'.

Clarissa ignored him and turned her attention again to the quivering Griffin. 'That boy is the best thing in my life, and if you and your helicopter have harmed a blade of hair on his head, I swear I'll … I'll …' She couldn't think of a punishment that would be harsh enough.

But luckily for Clarissa, she didn't have to, because at that moment she heard Frank's voice. 'CLARISSA! Conor's here! He's fine and so are the others!'

Frank was climbing down the side of the bridge, onto its ornate supporting pillars, and underneath he could see, clinging onto the beams below, Charlie, Damian and Gulliver. With them, holding on tight with huge, muscled arms was the massive fur-clad figure of Ogg, and gripping onto Ogg's legs … was Conor.

The guards (the ones who weren't bundling a grumbling Professor Griffin and his colleagues from the Snetterton Museum of Natural History into the back of the police cars) joined together with Frank and Clarissa to pull the scouts out from under O'Connell Bridge to safety. It took seven guards to pull Ogg out.

After Clarissa and Frank had hugged Conor and kissed him and checked that he and Charlie and the others weren't injured, they stood in front of Ogg.

Frank stuck out his hand and shook Ogg's warmly. 'You saved Clarissa's boy. Thank you,' he said.

'You are most welcome,' said the caveman.

Clarissa hugged Ogg tightly and kissed him on the elbow, which was as far up as she could reach.

'Mum, Frank – I'd like you to meet Ogg,' said Conor. 'Ogg the caveman.'

'I couldn't care less if you are a caveman, a milkman or a spaceman,' said Clarissa. 'Frank told me that Conor has been letting you stay in the dog's kennel while I have been working. After what you have done, you are welcome to stay with us as long as you like, and not in the kennel – our home is your home.'

Ogg smiled a gigantic, wide smile. Conor hugged his mum and then hugged Frank. Charlie started to cry, and Ogg put his big arms around all four of them.

Gulliver and Damian were standing to one side and watching the scene when Dennis and the rest of the scouts arrived. The scouts looked in wonder at the crashed helicopter. 'I hope they had insurance,' said Dennis to nobody in particular.

Gulliver, looking at Ogg and the others hugging, began to smile and snivel at the same time. Let's call it 'smivelling'.

'Oh, dry up, Gulliver,' said Damian, and then joined in, having a good smivel himself.

CHAPTER SEVENTEEN
FAMILY TREE

The next weekend, Clarissa and Conor had a big barbecue party at their house on Clobberstown Crescent. It seemed like everyone in Clobberstown was invited, and the back garden, front garden and every room in the house were full of happy, chatty people.

Ogg was the chef and was cooking up a storm on a barbecue he had built from rocks in the back garden, next to the new stone hut he had built beside the big oak tree at the back wall. Inside the hut he had painted the walls with pictures of his Stone Age wife and children.

On long trestle tables borrowed from the neighbours, the partygoers sat down to eat delicious burgers, steaks and sausages, all cooked to perfection by Ogg. The scout troop, Dennis Deegan, guards from Clobberstown Station, school friends, Ms. Sniffles and Ms. Hennigan all raised their glasses as Conor stood up to propose a toast.

'To Uncle Ogg,' he said. 'You saved myself and Charlie, and Damian and Gulliver. You're the best and biggest and OLDEST friend I could ever ask for, and I'm so glad you're here to stay. Welcome to the family, Uncle Ogg!'

And then Frank surprised everyone, especially Conor's mum, with a proposal of his own. Getting down on one knee and taking a small velvet ring box out of his pocket, he said, 'Clarissa, nearly losing Conor has shown me how much this family means to me. I want to be part of it too. Will you marry me?'

The crowd cheered, banging on the trestle tables with the palms of their hands and making the plates of burgers and sausages jump up and down. Then they quieted down, listening for Clarissa's response.

'Yes,' said Clarissa. 'I think I'd love to, Frank.'

The cheering started again, louder than ever. Ms. Hennigan, in floods of happy tears, sidled over to Ogg and held his hand.

‘I can’t believe it,’ said Conor to Charlie. ‘A new uncle AND a new dad, all in one day!’

Ogg squeezed Ms. Hennigan’s small hand gently in his gi-normous one. *Wow*, he thought, *a new family.*

5:50 PM

… and that's the end of the story.

Well, *almost*.

You see, after all that happened, Ms. Hennigan (or Aisling, as I call her) and me kind of got together.

We bought the house next door to Conor, Clarissa and Frank, so we see them every single day. Since Clarissa gave up most of her jobs, she has *much* more time for her family and friends.

Charlie has dinner with us in our new house every Thursday and Saturday.

And we bought a dog. Well, not a dog, exactly. A WOLF CUB.

5:50 PM

We called him GRIFFIN, mainly because of his hairy ears. He comes with us on scout trips.

Oh. Didn't I say? I'm a scout leader now, just like Dennis.

I also learned how to speak properly. And how to write, too. (Ms. Hennigan, sorry, Aisling taught me how.)

She suggested a little project for me a while back – to write my memoirs. A book about how I got frozen in ice, was found by a boy and a girl, was chased by evil professors, and how I ended up the happiest caveman in Ireland.

I loved the idea, and I couldn't wait to start.

I called it … **CONOR'S CAVEMAN**.

And … I hope you enjoyed reading it as much as I enjoyed writing it!

Alan Nolan lives and works in Bray, County Wicklow, Ireland. He is co-creator (with Ian Whelan) of *Sancho* comic, which was shortlisted for two Eagle awards, and is the author and illustrator of *The Big Break Detectives Casebook*, the *Murder Can Be Fatal* series and *Fintan's Fifteen* (The O'Brien Press).

Special thanks to my eagle-eyed editor Nicola Reddy, Michael O'Brien, Emma Byrne, Ivan O'Brien and all at The O'Brien Press.

Extra-special thanks to the staff and students of Church of Ireland College of Education, the Arts Council and to Children's Books Ireland for their excellent Bringing 2 Book initiative.

And extra-extra-special thanks, as ever, to my long-suffering family, Rachel, Adam, Matthew and Sam.

WWW.CONORSCAVEMAN.COM

WWW.ALANNOLAN.IE

WWW.OBRIEN.IE